BACK TO
MR & MRS

BACK TO
MR & MRS

BY

SHIRLEY JUMP

⊚™ MILLS & BOON®
Pure reading pleasure

First published in Great Britain 2007
Large Print edition 2007
Harlequin Mills & Boon Limited,
Eton House, 18-24 Paradise Road,
Richmond, Surrey TW9 1SR

ISBN: 978 0 263 19486 9

Set in Times Roman 17½ on 22 pt.
16-0907-39372

Printed and bound in Great Britain
by Antony Rowe Ltd, Chippenham, Wiltshire

For the man I married, who fished my manuscript
out of the trash and insisted I follow my dream.
His support has given me the courage to make writing
my full-time job, even though I still whine about
deadlines and characters who refuse to co-operate.

A special thanks to the coffee shops in Indiana, who
have kept me sufficiently caffeined up, so that I work
instead of napping or perfecting my FreeCell skills.
In particular, thanks to the staff at The Grind, who
gave me an insider's view of how a great coffee shop
operates. All those lattes were research, honest.

CHAPTER ONE

IF HER HANDS HADN'T been covered in double chocolate chip cookie dough, Melanie Weaver would have slapped duct tape over her mouth to stop herself from doing it again.

Saying yes when she really meant no.

Even when she had the best intentions of refusing, that slithery yes word slipped out instead. "Do you want a slice of Great-Grandma's fruitcake?" "Can you call Bingo for the Ladies' Auxiliary?" "Don't you just love this orange sweater?"

She hated fruitcake, had grown tired of the "B-4 and After" jokes, and never wore orange. Yet every year, Great Grandma brought a rock-hard fruitcake to Christmas dinner and Melanie choked down a slice, praising the wrinkled dates and dried cherries. On Tuesday nights, she dutifully showed up at the Presbyterian Church and called out letters and numbers in a smoky room filled with frantic red-dotters. And in Melanie's closet, there were three orange sweaters, birthday presents from her aunt Cornelia, who took Melanie's compliment of a mango-colored afghan as sure evidence of love for the color.

So it stood to reason, based on her history of always saying the wrong word at the wrong time, that on a bright spring Friday morning she would accept an invitation to her twenty-year class reunion when her life was as jumbled as a ten-thousand-piece puzzle.

"It'll be wonderful to have you!" Jeannie Jenkins, former cheerleader, blasted Melanie out of her reverie with a voice that hit unnatural decibels on the phone. "Everyone is, like, so looking forward to seeing you. I just knew, when I saw your name on the list, that you'd want to go. I mean, you must have just forgotten to RSVP or something."

"Or something," Melanie said. She hadn't returned the card because she hadn't intended to go, nor to answer all those questions about where Cade was.

Or, worse, see Cade there with another woman on his arm. She may be ending her marriage, but she wasn't quite ready to imagine him with someone else.

"The reunion is only, like, a week away. We'll all be together again, in just a few days. Isn't that so exciting?"

"Absolutely." Melanie tried to work some enthusiasm into her voice. She wanted to see her old friends, to catch up on their lives, but the thought of running into Cade, surrounded by memories of happier days, was unbearable. Her resolve would falter, and all those maybes would pop up, the same maybes that had stalled her leaving over and over again because she'd thought things might change. Go back to the way they were.

Either way, there was no return to those days. Melanie had changed, and Cade hadn't accepted those changes. She now had her shop, her new life. A life that no longer included Cade.

It was early afternoon and Cuppa Life was empty, save for Cooter Reynolds, who was sipping his daily mocha latte while reading the *Lawford News* and tapping his foot along with the soft jazz on the sound system. She had an hour until the college student flood poured into her coffee shop on the west side of Lawford, Indiana. And hopefully, only about five seconds until her daughter, Emmie, who worked part-time in the shop, was here for her Thursday shift. Melanie had started the cookies, sure Emmie would be in any second, but twenty minutes had passed since Emmie's shift was due to start and she still wasn't here.

"Did you like, go to college?" Jeannie didn't wait for an answer. "Me, I totally couldn't go. I was *so* done with school when it was over. The last thing I wanted was *more.*" She let out a dramatic sigh, as if Westvale High had been the equivalent of a stint in San Quentin.

Jeannie continued chattering on about how hard high school had been, how much she'd hated sophomore grammar, how the guidance counselor had tried to talk her into at least a two-year degree.

The words struck a note of pain in Melanie's chest. Ever since she'd been a kid, Melanie had dreamed of owning her own business.

She'd spent her summers here in Indiana, working in this very space, helping her grand-parents run what had then been a very suc-cessful antiques shop. Her grandfather, who'd seen that spark of entrepreneurial spirit, had encouraged Melanie to go to school and get a degree in business.

Melanie had had a scholarship to Notre Dame—a free ride to the college of her choice—and then been sidetracked by marriage, a child. Always, Cade had said, there would be time for Melanie—until her chance came up and he'd dismissed it faster than a perpetually tardy employee.

But Melanie refused to be put off. When Emmie was grown, Melanie had started taking night classes in business, working part-time at the Indianapolis university's coffee shop.

There, she had found her calling. In the camaraderie and coffee, she'd laughed more, looked forward to her days, and started thinking of that future she'd put on hold.

After leaving Cade, she'd moved to Lawford and opened her own coffeehouse, to create that community atmosphere in the city's busy business district. She'd gotten her certification as a barista at a conference for coffee shop owners and put those business classes to work.

It may not have been the dorm life and college experience she'd dreamed of during high school, but that didn't matter. She wouldn't have traded those years of raising Emmie for credit hours and a degree.

Emmie had been worth every sacrifice, ten times over. Her giggles, her first day of pre-school, her scraped knees and bicycle riding attempts. Even the early years with Cade had been wonderful, filled with laughter and meals eaten while sitting on the floor of their sparse apartment living room, with candle-light providing the mood and pillows serving as furniture.

Melanie shook off the thoughts and concentrated on stirring chocolate chips into the already chocolate dough, while Jeannie chattered on about how cool the reunion would be, how awesome it would be to reconnect with the other Westvale Highers. Jeannie was clearly a woman who didn't need much oxygen.

"So whatcha been doing all these years?" Jeannie asked when she came up for air, her voice interrupted by a blank sound in the phone line. "Oh, damn. Can you hold on a sec? I have another call, probably from ex number-two." Jeannie clicked off to retrieve Call Waiting.

Melanie pictured her personal resume: thirty-seven-year-old woman, almost divorced, running a coffee shop that had finally started showing a profit three months ago. Experience included nineteen years of running a vacuum and a dishwasher. Hey, but she could Calgon with the best of them.

It had been a conscious decision—the only decision she could imagine making—once she saw those two pink lines three weeks after prom night. She remembered being excited and scared, all at the same time. But Cade—and, oh, how she missed that old Cade sometimes—Cade had held her and told her it would all be okay. They'd work through this life twist together.

So she'd married him, had Emmie and then stayed home while Cade worked and went to law school. Later, she'd hosted the dinner parties, sent the thank-you notes and held down the home fort while Cade worked his way up the Fitzsimmons, Matthews and Lloyd ladder.

"Melanie?" Jeannie again, back from her other call. "You still there?"

"Yep." Finished with the cookie batter, Melanie stepped to the right and peeked around the corner of the shop and chuckled. Cooter had fallen asleep on one of the sofas, the paper across his chest, his snores providing an undertow of rhythm to the soft sounds of the stereo system.

"Remember Susan Jagger? She was saludadorian," Jeannie said, mangling the word, "and can you believe she started her own business selling dog sweaters? She's about to hit two million in sales! Oh, and remember Matt Phillips, the kid who always sat in the back and never said a word? He's, like, a famous software nerd now, like that Gates guy. I didn't really listen when he was telling me. I mean, it was *computers*." Jeannie paused to inhale. "And you, why I bet you've, like, invented a cure for cancer or something."

"Not quite." Melanie shouldn't be envious that other people had accomplished more than she had.

But she was. Green as the Jolly Green Giant.

Admitting she'd spent the last two decades helping her husband succeed seemed…embarrassing for someone who had been voted Most Likely to Become President and even more, a woman who had graduated in the top ten of her class.

"Then what *are* you doing?"

Melanie drew in a breath. So what if she wasn't running a huge company. Cuppa Life was something to be proud of. It was hers, all hers, and every inch of its success was due to Melanie, no one else.

She'd done it—opened a business and survived that critical first year. Sure, she was running an espresso machine instead of a mul- timillion dollar business, but she was happy. And that, she'd found, was all that mattered.

"I own a coffee shop in Lawford," Melanie said. "It's doing really well."

"Well, that's cool," Jeannie said, the words coming out with that exaggerated care that spelled unimpressed. "Like, everyone drinks coffee."

Melanie dropped cookie dough balls onto the sheets, refusing to let Jeannie's tone get her dander up.

"Anyway, I was, like, at the state courthouse the other day. Had a little incident with my neighbor's underwear." Jeannie let out a dramatic sigh. "Long story."

"I bet," Melanie said, biting back a laugh as she slid the first two cookie sheets into the oven. She peeked around the corner again for Emmie, who was now thirty minutes late.

"And while I was there," Jeannie continued, "I ran into Cade. He was doing some kind of lawyer thing. We got to talking and I told him I didn't have your RSVP, and he gave me your number here. So, we owe our little reuniting all to Cade!"

Melanie's breath got caught somewhere between her windpipe and her lungs. When would the mention of Cade's name stop doing that? She no longer loved him, hadn't in a long time, and shouldn't be affected by his voice, the sight of him or a discussion about the man she was about to divorce.

But some part of her, that leftover teenage romantic that had believed in happily ever after, still reacted. Still wanted him and still thought about him when the night closed in and loneliness served as her blanket.

"Anyway, he said you two were still together. Ever since high school. I think that's *so* romantic." Jeannie sighed. "You guys, like, give people hope."

The oven door, released from Melanie's grasp, shut with a slam.

"Still together?" Melanie echoed. How could he? He'd received the divorce papers. Seen her walk out the door a year ago. Except for the occasional conversation about Emmie and seeing him at a distance on the sidelines of Emmie's college soccer games, there had been nothing between them. Melanie had done everything she could to send the message it was over.

Clearly Cade hadn't been listening.

"Here I can't even hold onto a man for five minutes," Jeannie said. "I don't know how you do it." She took in a breath. "You guys got married so fast after graduation, then moved to what, Indianapolis? I don't blame you. When we were kids, we might as well have lived in

Mars, what with Westvale so far out in corn cob country. So, did you guys have any kids?"

"Yes, one. But, Jeannie, listen—"

Jeannie barreled on, not even hearing her. "You guys are, like, my idols. I'm divorced, twice now, soon to be three times. But it's not so bad. The alimony is almost like a full-time job." Jeannie laughed. "Anyway, you must have the coolest husband in the world. Especially if you stuck with him and had a rug rat."

At that word, Melanie heard the bell over the entrance to Cuppa Life jingle. She peeked around the corner again, and smiled. Enter one rug rat, or rather, a nineteen-year-old-sweetheart named Emmie.

"Hi, Mom," Emmie said as she headed into the kitchen.

"You deserve it, Melanie," Jeannie was saying. "I mean, like, *someone* should get the fairy tale ending. Besides Snow White. That girl never even changed her dress in the whole movie. I mean, what man wants that? Like, wouldn't she start to smell?"

"Jeannie, Cade and I—"

"Oh, almost time for my manicure! I need to get to the salon."

Melanie looked down at her own hands, glistening with butter. There was dough under her short, no-nonsense nails and in the creases of her knuckles.

She needed to tell Jeannie the truth. That Melanie and Cade, the "it" couple at Westvale High, had fallen prey to the divorce statistics. Melanie had ended up pregnant at eighteen, married and living in a cramped apartment in Indianapolis before her nineteenth birthday. That she was changing diapers and figuring out the best way to potty train before she was old enough to drink.

That *Cade* had been the one to go on to

school, thanks to his father funding the tuition and providing a part-time job at the family law firm to cover other expenses. Cade had been the one to rise to the top of his field, with Melanie by his side, providing that home front support.

Since then, her biggest accomplishment had been learning how to make a good latte.

Well, that and Emmie, she thought as her daughter came into the small kitchen area, pressed a quick kiss to her mother's cheek, then slid into place beside her to help with the rest of the cookies. Emmie was tall and lithe, with the same blond hair as her mother, but the wide, deep eyes of her father. She had Cade's athleticism, Melanie's wit, and on most days, a sweet, compassionate way about her that had survived the ugly teen years. She was Cade and Melanie's pride and joy—

The one thing they had done right together.

Yet, since the separation, Emmie had become more distant, more rebellious. Her short cropped hair was now topped with red, her ears tripled in earrings and her attitude less friendly and more filled with annoyance.

Jeannie sighed. "I *so* wish I'd had that kind of happy ending, too."

As Melanie opened her mouth to tell Jeannie the truth, it somehow got lodged in her throat. Maybe it was pride, maybe it was the thought of everyone in her graduating class giving her that pitying look at the reunion, as if she hadn't measured up to their expectations.

Or maybe it was simply that she had yet to take off her wedding ring.

The ring fit tight, considering she'd gained a couple dozen pounds in the years of marriage. That was all. It certainly wasn't because somewhere deep in her heart, she

EPILOGUE

The priest nods at me and I hand my son to Angela in order that he can be named before God in the ivory silk gown I never wore, but which Frances had brought with her in order that I am the last generation to be skipped.

After thirty years of me never having entered church, this is the second service that I have attended within the last year, the first having taken place in Granada last week, when we bade our final farewell to Jessie. Although this is a happy occasion, I can hear Frances's sobs in the echo stone, and I look around as the priest takes young Jack from the arms of his mother.

The priest makes a cross with holy water on the head of my son, incanting in an ancient tongue that is joined by the screams of a soul who is recognized by God and the Church, and out of this fusion of voices comes a terrible sound. A stone-cracking shot rings out in the church, echoes and spills from the darkness, through the open door and onto the promontory of cliff.

Elvira flinches, reaches quickly and surely into her handbag, as if this is something she has been waiting for. Outside, screams rise from the sea like the mad soundings of flocks of gulls and a ripple ebbs then flows through the church as friends and family laugh hysterical relief.

Through the arch doorway of the church I can see a thin strip of land and then sea, a boat bobbing in the swell, full of waving villagers under the falling fire of gunpowder. Into a big sky, my son's countrymen have launched a firework commemoration of the soundings of baptism.

THE END

clasped, beaming at each other, thinking nothing and no one would ever separate them.

They'd been wrong.

"Uh, Mom?" Emmie said, her voice now an urgent whisper as she put on a pair of oven mitts and switched out baked cookies for her loaded sheet of dough. "When I needed a ride to work, the only person available was—"

The door to the kitchen swung open and for the second time in five minutes, Melanie drew in a sharp breath that became a block in her windpipe.

Cade.

He entered the small kitchen, seeming to take up half the space without even trying. Melanie swallowed hard, surprised by the instantaneous, explosive gut reaction to her husband.

Correction: almost ex-husband.

Apparently her hormones hadn't received the separation papers, nor read over the draft of the divorce agreement, because they were still screaming attraction.

And why wouldn't they? Cade hadn't changed at all in the year they'd been apart. A few more crinkles around his blue eyes, the perpetual worry line above his dark brows etched a little deeper, but overall he was as handsome as he had been when she'd still loved him. He may be a bit disheveled by the stress of his day, but he was still sexy.

Really sexy. Familiar desire rose inside her, coupled with the longing to touch his face, run a hand down his chest, feel the security of his long, lean body against hers. The temperature in the room seemed to multiply. Melanie pulled at the neck of her T-shirt and checked the air conditioner. Nothing broken there—

Except for her resolve.

Attraction, though, had never been their problem. Marriages weren't based solely on the swirling, tangling pulses of estrogen and testosterone. They needed communication, understanding, give and take.

And a man who wanted more for his wife than perfecting her baked Alaska and diaper changing.

Cade still sported the same athletic physique—trim, broad-shouldered, a chest of hard, tight planes. It had never been solely his body that had attracted Melanie, though she hadn't minded the nice physical package that had wrapped around Cade.

It had been his eyes. And his smile.

Right now, the smile was absent, but those eyes—the same big blue eyes that had drawn her attention that first day in freshman year, standing in the hall outside Mrs. Owen's art class—they now riveted her attention for a brief, taut second, before she remembered the man may have incredible eyes, but horrible husband skills. He'd never listened to her, not really, never heard her when she talked about *her* dreams, *her* goals. He'd been as focused as a horse with blinders, seeing only one road ahead—for both of them.

And when it had really mattered, Cade hadn't been there at all.

The oven timer dinged. Cookies. She needed to tend to the cookies. Melanie grabbed a spatula and a pot holder, but her attention was still all on Cade, not the hot pan she withdrew from the oven.

"Melanie?" Jeannie asked, her voice concerned, seeming to come from a thousand miles away. "I really have to get to the salon, but I wanted to be sure you and Cade can do me this eensy weensy favor. You will do it, right?"

"Hi, Melanie," Cade said, his voice the same deep baritone she'd known for more than half her life. Once upon a time, that sound had made her heart sing. "Is it okay if I stay here for a bit?" he said. "I've got some time to kill before a meeting."

"Yes, yes, of course," Melanie said. And promptly dropped the spatula. It landed on the vinyl floor with a soft clatter.

"Oh, great!" Jeannie cried. "I'll see you a week from Friday then!" She giggled. "You and Cade. It'll be the best speech *ever.* You guys always did have a way with words. And a lot more." She let out another laugh, then hung up.

"No! I meant to say no!" Melanie yelled into the phone, scrambling for the spatula, but Jeannie was already gone, off for some French tips.

The yes had been for Cade, not Jeannie. Somehow, the sight of him after so much time apart had knocked her off-kilter. As it had in the early days, before their "way with words" became more about flinging them around the living room in arguments that went nowhere.

Emmie tossed her mother a grin, then turned away and started sliding the cookies onto the cooling rack. Melanie tossed the spatula into the sink, all thumbs and as consternated as a chicken in a fox den.

She grabbed a warm chocolate chip cookie off the wire cooling rack and stuffed it in her mouth before she could make the same mistake twice—

Say yes when she really meant to say no.

CHAPTER TWO

As HIS DAUGHTER HANDED him a cup of coffee, Cade watched the woman he'd once thought he knew better than himself hurry between the espresso machine and the bakery case, greeting customers by name, laughing at their jokes, dispensing coffee with a happy, friendly cheer—and wondered for the thousandth time when they had slipped off their common track.

Somewhere between "I do" and "I don't," something had gone wrong in his marriage. He was a corporate lawyer. His specialty was fixing tangled legal messes. Why couldn't he fix the one in his own house?

He'd tried, Lord knew he'd tried, but

Melanie had thrown up a wall and refused to remove a single chink in the brick.

God, he missed her. Every morning, he woke up to an empty space in his bed and an ache in his chest that no painkiller could soothe. At night, the talking heads on TV kept him company instead of the soft tones of Melanie, telling him about her day, about something Emmie had said or done.

He took a seat at one of the tables, watching his wife's lithe, fluid movements. She was still as beautiful as the day he'd married her. A little heavier, but over the years he'd found he liked the extra weight on her hips and waist, the fullness in her breasts. The womanly curves had always held a magical comfort, soothing him at the end of a stressful day.

Always, Melanie had been there, supporting him in those early days when it seemed he'd never rise above the minion position of law clerk.

He poured sugar into his cup. It dissolved as easily as the bonds of his marriage.

Still, he'd put off signing the papers that would file their divorce. He had hope, damn it, that this could be fixed. That he could broker a mutually satisfactory agreement, a return to business as usual, something he had done a thousand times between warring corporations.

Every time he looked at Melanie, a constant smile curved across her face as she chatted and poured, the ache in his chest quadrupled. Need for her—not just sexual need, but an indefinable, untouchable need that ran bone-deep—stirred in his gut, rushing through his veins. He wanted to take her in his arms, hold her to his chest and kiss her until he made this past year go away.

But deep in his heart he knew they'd gone

way beyond the point where a simple kiss could solve anything.

"Dad," Emmie said, coming over to him. Now a college sophomore, Emmie had the same heart-shaped face and delicate features as her mother, except now her hair was spiked, her lips painted a dark crimson. "Sit at the counter. It's way more comfortable."

Before he could protest, his daughter had taken his cup of Kenyan roast and put it on the laminate surface. Three feet from Melanie. He and Melanie exchanged a quick, knowing glance.

Obviously she knew Emmie was trying to bring them together. Why shouldn't she? Emmie hadn't asked for the divorce and she'd made it clear she didn't like alternating between her two parents' homes for weekly dinners and occasional laundry stops, like a perpetual ping-pong game.

Cade sure as hell wasn't happy watching his marriage whittle away, either.

He rose and crossed to the wooden bar, settling onto one of the cushioned stools. "You've created a nice place here."

He hadn't seen his wife in a year and that was the best he could come up with? This is *nice?*

After this, he was heading to the bookstore to see if there was a *Resurrecting Your Marriage for Dummies.* Because clearly this dummy was failing at Wooing Back a Wife 101.

"Thanks," Melanie said. She wiped off the steamer spout, then tossed the dirty cloth into a bucket of laundry inside the kitchen. She washed her hands and picked up the rack of freshly baked cookies and began loading them into the glass case, arranging them as carefully as she used to arrange the pillows in their living room.

"Is it going well?" Cade asked. "From what I've seen, this place is as popular as an elf at Christmas."

She laughed. "Things are going much better than expected."

He heard the undertones of their last fight in those two sentences. Cade was smart enough to back away from that. "I'm happy for you, Melanie."

Emmie brushed by him, giving him an elbow hint. "Say something, Dad," she whispered.

Cade held up his hands and looked to Emmie for help. She gave him the duh look she'd perfected by her sixteenth birthday. Oh, yeah, he was the dad. He was supposed to have all the answers.

He did—all but this one.

Cade shifted on the stool. "Are you going to tease your hair and unearth that Kiss concert T-shirt for Friday night?"

She chuckled. "Oh gosh, that was a thousand years ago. I don't think I saved the shirt."

"You did. Bottom drawer, on the right." He knew, because he'd been in their dresser after she'd left, looking for something, and come across the worn image of Gene Simmons. For a moment, Cade had been back there, in the thirtieth row, rocking along with Melanie as they held up a lighter during a ballad and sang along until their voices cracked.

"I remember that night," she said softly, then shook her head and got busy with the cookies again. "Anyway, it doesn't matter because I'm not going to the reunion. I'll have to save the Aqua Net for another night."

She'd tried to pass it off as a joke, but Cade wasn't laughing. "Didn't you just tell Jeannie you would go?" He gestured toward the phone. "I couldn't help but overhear. Jeannie's voice is like a bullhorn."

"I only said yes to—"

"Get her off your back?" He chuckled, reaching for that light, easy feeling again. It seemed to flit in and out, as ungraspable as a moth. "I know the feeling. It's why I said yes, too."

Emmie headed into the back of the shop, to get supplies or something, Cade supposed. As soon as their daughter was out of earshot, Melanie stopped working on the cookies, leaned an arm over the glass case and glared at him. "Why did you tell Jeannie we were still together?"

"I think there's still a chance to work this out. You don't throw nineteen years away on a whim."

"You think this was a *whim?*" She shook her head, then lowered her voice. "It was the hardest decision I have ever made."

Hurt stabbed at his chest, thinking of how

quickly she'd been gone, how fast she'd escaped her half of their life. "I doubt that."

She let out a gust of frustration. "Sign the papers, Cade. It's over."

"No." He slipped off the stool and came around to the back of the glass case. "I'm done catwalking around the issue, biding my time. Thinking all you needed was a little space. I want answers, Mel, a solution." He drew within inches of her. "Tell me what went wrong so I can change it."

She threw up her hands. "Our marriage isn't a clock, Cade. You can't replace a couple gears and call it good as new."

"And you can't just throw it out because you wanted a better model."

"That isn't why I left." Melanie circled the counter and began wiping down the case's glass with an ammonia-scented cleaner and a white cotton cloth. An old man snored lightly on the sofa across the room, the paper on his torso fluttering as his chest rose up and down. "We made a mistake," she said under her breath. "Why can't you just let it go?"

"Because I still love you." The words tore from his throat, contained in his chest for so long, fenced in by a hope that grew dimmer with every day Melanie refused his calls, ignored his e-mails, refused his requests to talk.

She shook her head and when she did, he saw the glimmer of tears in her eyes. "You don't even know me."

I would if you'd give me a chance, he wanted to scream. *Let me try again. Don't take away the one rock I've always stood on.*

Before he could say anything, the bell rang and a woman in a business suit strode into the small shop and up to the register. Emmie came out of the back, headed to the register and greeted the woman, but her attention, Cade knew, was half on her parents.

Melanie took out some of her frustrations on the glass case, scrubbing it until it gleamed like silver. As her left hand rose up to swipe away a smear, a glint caught Cade's eye.

Her wedding ring.

The same plain gold band he'd slipped on her finger in the county courthouse nearly twenty years ago.

A wave of hope rose within him, but he held it back. Cade was nothing if not a practical man. His wife may still be wearing her ring, but she'd gone back to using her maiden name and hadn't slept in his bed for over a year. A piece of jewelry didn't mean anything.

And yet, he hoped like hell it did.

"Mellie," he said, slipping into the habit of her nickname. He grabbed her hand, stopping her from cleaning the glass into oblivion. He lowered his voice and turned so that the customer—and Emmie—couldn't see or overhear them. "Go with me to the reunion. Wear that T-shirt and that bright pink lipstick you used to love. Go back in time with me, for one night. We could go out to dinner first, talk—"

"About what, Cade?" A glimmer washed over the deep thunderstorm of green in her eyes. Behind them, Emmie watched out of the corner of her eye, her movements quiet and small as she finished the customer's latte and poured the steamed milk into a paper cup emblazoned with the bright crimson Cuppa Life logo.

Melanie noticed their daughter's interest and led Cade into the small kitchen space, letting the door shut behind them. The close quarters only quadrupled Cade's awareness of Melanie, of the way her chest rose and fell with each breath, the silky blond tendrils drifting about her shoulders, the jeans hugging her hips.

He wanted to kiss her, to close the gap between them. If only a simple meeting of their bodies would be enough to bridge the chasm. But even Cade knew it wasn't that simple.

"Talk about what?" she repeated. "About how I failed you?" she said. "As a wife, a mother? About how you were at work—always at work—even when I needed you most?"

Regret slammed into his gut. He didn't want to think about that day. Ever.

It was the one tape he couldn't rewind. Couldn't delete. Couldn't do over. "Melanie, I've said I was sorry a hundred times."

She sighed. "It's not about being sorry, Cade, it's about changing what got us there in the first place."

"That doesn't work if only one of us is

trying," he countered. "And I'm trying damn it. Go with me, Mel. For one night be my wife again."

"I can't put on that show anymore." She held her ground, arms crossed over her chest. "Besides, did Jeannie tell you she wanted us to make a speech?"

"Isn't that supposed to be the class president's thing?"

"She thought it would be..." Her voice trailed off.

"Be what?" Cade asked, leaning closer, inhaling the scent of her skin, the sweetness of fresh-baked cookies, of the woman he'd lived with more than half his life. "Would be what, Melanie?" Cade whispered, his mouth so close to hers, all it would take was a few inches of movement to kiss her. To have her in his arms, against his heart.

"Romantic," she said after a minute, expelling a disgusted sigh on the word. "The whole Prom King and Queen still together thing."

He moved back a step. "But we aren't, are we?"

She shook her head, resolute. "No, we're not."

The need for her smoldered inside him, a wildfire ready to erupt. He still loved her, damn it, and refused to let her quit so easily.

His gaze traveled down, to her lips, her jaw, the delicate arch of her throat. The old attraction that had simmered between them for more than twenty years ignited anew in his chest, the embers never really extinguished.

He wanted her, Lord, did he want her. He wanted to sweep her off her feet, carry her out of this shop and back to their bed. Every fiber in his being ached to feel her familiar, sweet body beneath his, to lose himself inside her, to find that connection he'd never found anywhere else.

A slight flush crept into Melanie's cheeks, warming them to cotton-candy-pink. She opened her mouth, shut it again, then reached for a spoon, succeeding only in knocking it along the counter. It skittered under a display stand of teas. Was she thinking the same thing?

Then it was gone, and she was back to all business. "The idea of going together and pretending we're still together is—"

"Insane," he finished.

Melanie reached for a towel, folding, then unfolding and refolding it, a nervous habit he recognized—and also a sign of hope. Maybe not much, but he'd take whatever he could get.

"Completely insane," she said, watching him, her eyes as unreadable as the Pacific. Her hand stilled, the towel limp in her grip.

A breath hitched between them. Another. Cade's grip curled around the countertop, willpower keeping him from reaching out and pulling her to him.

"If we don't go, or if we go separately, everyone's going to know we're getting…" He left off the word, still unable to believe it was going to happen. It was why he had yet to even look at the divorce paperwork. Seeing the word, speaking it, would make it a reality.

And Cade sure wasn't ready to let go yet.

"Divorced," Melanie finished. The eight letters that were changing Cade's life hung between them, as bright as a neon sign.

"Yeah." His marriage was so far off track—hell, they weren't even on the same cross-country route anymore—that he wondered if there was even a chance of getting it back to where it had been.

"I should probably get back to work," she said, folding the towel one last time before leaving it on the counter.

"I hear you're thinking about expanding this place," Cade said, changing tactics, avoiding the dreaded "D" word.

Someday, he'd have to deal with it. Just not today.

"How did you…?" Surprise flitted across Melanie's delicate features, then disappeared when she realized the daughter outside the kitchen was the source of the information. "Yes, I am planning an expansion."

"As in a mini-mall or world domination of the cappuccino industry?"

She laughed. "Nothing that big." Then her brows knitted together and she studied him. "Do you really want to know?"

He nodded. Was that what it was? He had stopped listening and she had stopped talking? "I do."

"Do you promise not to give me a list of pros and cons?"

He winced at the memory, then put up two fingers. "Scout's honor."

She laughed, the merry sound such sweet music to his ears. "You were never a Boy Scout."

He grinned. "I always had Boy Scout intentions, though."

"I remember," Melanie said quietly.

"I do, too." The memory slipped between them, the shared thought coming easily, as if they shared a brain. Their first date. A car broken down on the side of the road. Two elderly ladies standing outside of the Mazda, looking confused and helpless. Rain pelting down on Cade's head as he filled their radiator with a jug of water he kept in his trunk, then put a temporary duct tape patch on the leaking hose.

Melanie had called him a Boy Scout, then, when the women were gone, drawn him to her, her lips soft and sweet. He'd have rebuilt fifty transmissions that night if he'd known a simple act of kindness would turn Mellie's interest in him from mild to five-alarm hot.

"You wanted to hear my plans," Melanie said, interrupting his thoughts.

Cade recovered his wits. "Yes, I would."

"Okay. It's slow and I could use a break. Let's go in the back." As the customer lingered, asking about the different types of muffins, Melanie poured herself a cup of coffee, then gestured to Cade to follow her to the rear of the shop, where she'd set up a cozy nook with two leather love seats. It was a small area, but the bronze wash on the walls and the deep chocolate sofas made it inviting and warm. Melanie always had had great decorating skills.

She and Cade took seats on opposite sofas, a few feet away from the armchair holding

Rip Van Winkle. "My plan is to double the space," she said, laying her cup on the end table. "Add some game tables, a children's play area, build a room for business people to hold meetings. Maybe even add a stage for open mike nights." Excitement brightened her eyes. He got the feeling she wanted to tell someone, to maybe…just maybe, get his take on her idea.

In the old days, before Emmie had come along, Melanie had been filled with ideas, their evenings in that dingy apartment passing quickly with energetic conversations about what could be if they took this path or that path. In the end, there'd only been one road to follow. Cade had always thought it was the right one, but now, seeing his wife's enthusiasm, he wondered if he'd missed a detour.

Beside them, the old man snarfled in his sleep. "Bad deer," he muttered.

Each of them laughed quietly at the non sequiter, providing a moment of détente, connection. Then Melanie cleared her throat and directed her attention to the room. "Anyway, we're really cramped in our four hundred square feet here. I figured if I could get a bit more space, I'd get more of the college crowd. The building next door is up for sale and the owner has already offered it to me. If I could buy it, knock down this wall—" she gestured toward the plaster finish "—I'd double the space."

He let out a low whistle, impressed. The Melanie he knew had been intelligent, witty, cool under pressure—but never had he seen this business savvy part of her. "You've taken this place a lot further than I thought it could go when we looked at it last year, after you inherited it from your grandparents. I guess I didn't see the potential then."

She studied the brass studs on the armrest's seam. "No, you didn't."

A pair of size fifty boots had a smaller heel than Cade. Had he crushed her dream? He'd only been trying to be pragmatic, to steer her away from a potential mistake. Clearly he'd done the opposite. "I'm sorry, Melanie."

She didn't meet his gaze. Instead she smoothed a hand over the leather. "It's in the past. I'm all about moving forward."

The implied word—alone. "You have a lot of plans for this place. For that you need additional funding, right?"

She nodded.

"Something that's hard to get when you're a relatively new business." From Emmie, he knew she'd financed the opening of the shop on her own, with a little from her grandparent's inheritance, the rest from the nice folks at Visa.

"Tell me about it," Melanie said, clearly

frustrated. "Banks want me to have years of success under my belt before they'll lend me any money. But I can't get those years of success without investing in my business. It's that old Catch-22."

It was also an area he knew well—and an opportunity to help. And maybe, just maybe, she'd let him in again. At this point, Cade would knock down the damned wall himself if he thought it would help defrost the glacier between them.

"I have a proposition for you," Cade said, deciding he wasn't going to let his marriage go without a fight. He could only pray this was an offer Melanie couldn't refuse.

CHAPTER THREE

"WHAT DO YOU MEAN—a proposition?" she asked.

Cade rose, slipped over to her love seat and sat down beside her, not too close, but close enough that their conversation couldn't be overheard by the snoring man or the woman still hemming and hawing about blueberry versus peach crumble.

He was also close enough to catch the vanilla scent on her skin, the same fragrance he always associated with Melanie. Like cookies, homemade bread…all the things he'd missed in his childhood and had found in his wife.

His wife.

Damn, he missed her. Missed coming home to her smile, missed holding her. Regardless of what that piece of paper on his desk said, he'd never stopped thinking of Melanie as his wife.

"If you stayed married to me…" Cade paused for a second, letting the last word linger in the air as the idea took root in his mind, "just for a while, you could get that funding a lot easier."

She backed up against the arm of the sofa, warding off his idea. "*No.* I want to do this on my own, Cade. *Without* your help or your family money."

He heard the seeds of the familiar argument taking hold in her tone. Eighteen months ago, they'd stood here in this very space, Cade glancing around at the dusty antiques, the cluttered room, seeing only years of books in the red, not potential. He'd offered to help, to give her the business guidance the place clearly needed, to invest some of the inheritance from his grandfather that had done nothing but sit in the bank, but she'd refused.

I want to do this on my own, Cade, she'd said then. *I don't need you to tell me what's wrong. I just want you to say go for it and let me do it.*

Instead he'd pulled out a thick stack of research he'd done on the antique industry, statistics proving what worked—and what didn't. She'd shoved the papers back at him, and in doing so, shut the first door on their marriage.

He'd shut the second one himself.

He tossed her a grin. "Just think of it as a little payback for all the years you helped me."

She rose, frustration running through every inch of her face. "Where is this new and improved Cade coming from? Since when did you want me to be all independent?"

He blinked. "I never said you had to be

some Stepford wife, Mellie. I've always wanted you to have your own life."

"As long as it wasn't at the expense of yours." Melanie took in a breath, erasing the quick flash of hurt in her eyes. "Cade, you just don't understand how important it is for me to have something of my own. To do this *myself.*"

"I'm trying, Melanie." He paused, waiting until she sank back onto the seat beside him. "I promise not to do anything more than let you have my credit score," Cade continued. "We have a lot of assets together, Melanie, a financial record, a damned nice nest egg of Matthews money. The bank will look more favorably on your loan if—"

"If I pretend I'm still married to you."

"It's not pretending. We *are* married."

"Only because you won't sign the divorce papers."

"I've been busy."

She gave him the eye roll Emmie had inherited. She sighed, considering him for a long moment. "I'm not agreeing to anything. Not until I know what you want in exchange."

"Nothing."

She shook her head. "I know you, Cade. You don't make a deal without both sides gaining something. You help me get my loan, but what do you get?"

"Nothing, except—" he drew in a breath "—a date to the reunion."

In her green eyes, the thoughts connected. "As your wife, you mean."

Cade had brokered enough deals to know when he'd reached the crux, the point where the agreement could be broken by one party leaning too far or pushing too hard.

Melanie would eventually be awarded the divorce with or without his signature. He glanced at her left hand, at the circle of gold on her ring finger.

He weighed his next words, trying to figure out what wouldn't make Melanie bolt, or worse, encourage her to throw the countertop Capresso machine at his head. "Not as my wife," he lied, "more as a...fellow reunion attendee. Let people assume what they want." He voiced the idea as calmly as he would the terms of a corporate merger. Start with business-only, and pray like hell it turned into something more personal later.

Her gaze narrowed. "Why are you suddenly so interested in going to the class reunion? If I remember right, you skipped the fifth and the tenth. What's so big about the twentieth?"

Cade didn't miss a beat. "Bill Hendrickson."

"The kid who carried a briefcase to school every day?"

He nodded. "He's now the owner of one of

the largest law firms in the Midwest and he's looking for a new partner."

That much was true. For a month or so, Bill had been trying to meet with Cade, but their respective schedules had kept them from finding a common time. Bill suggested a quick meeting at the reunion. "Bring your wife," Bill had said, unaware of the rift in the Matthews marriage. "I'd love to introduce her to my Shelley."

Bill had made it clear he liked to employ family men because he thought they were more committed, more honorable. Cade wasn't so sure he agreed with Bill's logic, but he did know one thing for sure—he'd love to work for the massive, national firm that Bill headed. They'd handled clients Cade could only dream of working for; the kind with names that everyone in America knew.

It was what he'd worked for, toiling away

under his father's thumb, hoping to prove himself and then break into the big leagues.

"What's wrong with staying at Fitzsimmons, Matthews and Lloyd?" Melanie asked.

Cade's gaze swept over the hourglass shape of his wife, down the dusting of freckles that trailed a pattern from her shoulder to her wrist, a path he'd kissed more than once. The ache that had become his constant companion in the last year tightened its grip. "Because I need a change of pace."

If this divorce happened—and as more time went by with Melanie remaining resolute in her plans, he knew it would—then he knew he'd have to leave. He couldn't stand living twenty minutes from Melanie, knowing she was moving on with her life.

And worst of all—dating other men.

He tore his gaze away from her. A woman as gorgeous and vivacious as Melanie wouldn't be going to bed alone for very long. "Bill's firm is in Chicago and—"

"You're moving to *Chicago?*" she said, her voice soft, surprised.

"I'm considering it, if everything goes well with Bill. Chicago is only a few hours away, which means I can still see Emmie." He grinned. "Half the time she's here or out with friends. I'm more of a laundry dump than a dad."

Melanie echoed his smile. "I know the feeling. She does the same thing to me. If I hadn't hired her, I don't think I'd see her for more than a five-minute conversation a month."

"Our little girl has grown up, hasn't she?" Cade's memory ran through a quick tape of Emmie's first steps, first day of school, first bike. The years had rocketed by too fast. Hindsight berated him for missing far too many of those firsts.

"Yeah," Melanie said, and the bittersweet expression on her face told him she was watching the same mental movie. "If you get the job, are you selling the house?"

Back to the logistics of divvying up a marriage. "I'll keep it for a while," Cade said. If there was a chance Melanie would ever live there again, would ever sit at the oak dining room table they'd bought for their fifth anniversary and share a dinner with him, he wanted to have that familiar three-bedroom in Indianapolis waiting.

He shook off the thought. Cade had to be pragmatic instead of getting caught up in the green of her eyes, the scent of her skin. The sheer magic of being so close to her again, separated only by a few inches of love seat.

This reunion idea was a last-ditch effort, brought about because he'd thought he'd read some meaning in the gold band on her left hand. Assuming, that was, that she'd ever loved him at all. That she hadn't married him just because she'd been pregnant with Emmie. In the still, dark night, *that* was the possibility that haunted Cade. Had he been so clueless, he'd imagined a love that had never existed?

"I had no idea you were considering a move," Melanie said.

"I haven't broken it to Emmie yet, so please don't tell her. I want to have something definite in hand first."

More, Cade needed to know for sure there was zero chance with his wife. All year, he'd kept telling himself that given a little time, Melanie would be back. She hadn't.

With all the signs she'd been sending him, he could have taken out a billboard: Your Marriage Is Over. And yet, the glutton in him continued to hope that the past nineteen years had formed a foundation they could come back to, build a new beginning on, after they moved the last few years of wreckage out of the way.

The realist in him whispered their foundation was made of sand, not stone.

"Oh." Melanie's mouth formed the vowel, held it for a minute, as if it was taking her a moment to get used to the idea of him moving away. "Okay."

"Anyway, you know how I hate to go to those things, especially alone," Cade said, putting on a smile, making his case, treading carefully. "I can never remember anyone's name. I need a wingman."

I need you.

It wasn't until Melanie responded with a smile of her own that Cade found himself able to breathe again. "You *are* pretty bad at that. Remember when you kept calling Jim Sacco 'Stan'?"

Cade laughed. "He was a former partner at

Fitzsimmons, Matthews and Lloyd, too. We even worked together a couple times. I've never lived that one down."

Melanie joined his laughter. Cade wished he could reach out, capture that sound in a jar and bring it home with him. The walls in the house had grown as silent as tombs without Melanie.

"Oh, and what about the time you forgot the name of the governor?" She chuckled softly. "So much for any political ambitions you might have had."

"That's when my wingman came in mighty handy," he said, thinking of that nightmare dinner party seven years ago, of Melanie slipping in with her easy touch and smoothing everything over. With them so close together on the love seat, it was almost like before. Cade and Melanie, staying up late, finishing off the appetizers while they rehashed the night. "You told him some story about me getting the flu or something—"

Another smile from her, the kind that could disrupt a man's best intentions. "And I told him the medicine had some kind of mental side effects."

"All that mattered was that he bought it and signed the firm as his personal counsel. *You* made that save, Mellie." He leaned forward, careful not to invade her personal space, to keep it casual, to act as if his heart didn't still trip over itself every time she smiled. "That's why I need you with me at the reunion. You make me look good."

"Oh, I don't know about that." Her glance flitted away. She reached for her coffee, her hand a nervous flutter that nearly toppled the cup. It clattered against the table, then settled into place.

"I'm serious. Your talent is people. Making

them feel comfortable, welcome." He glanced around the corner of their little nook, into the main part of Cuppa Life. The cozy coffee shop was beginning to fill with chattering college students, clustering around the tables and doing homework, playing cards, or just talking. It was the polar opposite to the stuffy, serious law offices of Fitzsimmons, Matthews and Lloyd. For a minute, he wondered what it was like to work in a place like this. To escape the daily grind of a job that had never felt quite right, as if all these years he'd been wearing the wrong size suit. "This place is 'Cheers' with caffeine."

She laughed. "Not quite as successful, but, yeah, I guess it does have that kind of atmosphere. Speaking of which, I better get back and help Emmie with the afternoon rush." She rose and turned to go.

Cade reached for her arm. Everything

within him begged for more contact, more of her. With reluctance he held back, tempered his touch to border on acquaintance, not spouse. "Melanie, go with me. Please."

She paused, her emerald gaze meeting his for a long, silent second. "Are you really moving to Chicago?"

Once again, the belt tightened around his heart. If this didn't work, there was no way Cade could stay in that house another second. "Yeah."

Emmie shouted to her mother that she needed help making something called a "Frazzle." With an apology, Melanie hurried back to the counter.

In a blur of activity, Melanie dumped a slew of ingredients into a blender and whirred the icy concoction together. She poured the frothy liquid into a cup, handed it to the customer, then set to work on a couple of lattes, filling the orders of the group of twenty-somethings who'd all come in at once. It was a good five minutes before she had a second to return to Cade.

He rehashed their conversation in his head, as if a replay could show him how to fine tune it next time, to get a different result.

"Did you mean what you said about helping me get my loan?" she said when she came back.

He nodded. "As much or as little as you want. I can even give you the money from our account."

She shook her head. "I want to do this alone."

"It's our money, Mel."

"It's *your* inheritance. I want to earn my own. I want this—" she indicated the shop "—to be mine."

"Okay. Whatever you want. You call all the shots, Melanie."

She hesitated so long, worry began to crowd onto Cade's shoulders.

Then she thrust out her hand. He took it, feeling the familiar delicate palm inside his much bigger one, knowing that if he inhaled the fragrance of her skin, he'd be swept back up into what could have been, instead of what really was.

Instead he shook when she did, the business-like stance feeling so odd, he wanted to laugh.

"Then you have a deal, Cade Matthews."

CHAPTER FOUR

"WHAT WAS I THINKING?" Melanie slumped into one of the bar stools beside Kelly Webber, a frequent customer turned good friend. The college crowd had begun petering out as night began to fall and discussion of dorm room parties replaced the complaints about professors with homework fetishes. Emmie was sitting at a table in the corner of the room, ostensibly doing her homework, but really chatting with a friend while their dueling laptops accessed Cuppa Life's wireless Internet connection.

Melanie let out a sigh. "Once again, I said yes when I should have said no."

"That's called Momitis. It's how I got roped into doing the PTL dinner and chairing the book drive all in the same week." Kelly took a sip from her decaf iced mocha and gave Melanie a sympathetic smile. She had her dark brown hair back in a ponytail and wore a blue track suit, her usual running-the-kids attire. Her two sons were taking karate lessons at the studio three doors down, giving Kelly a moment for a coffee and friendship break. "Just skip the reunion. Who needs that one-upmanship fest?"

"But Cade needs my help." Melanie sat back and blinked. "What am I saying? I'm not married to Cade anymore, or at least I won't be soon. I shouldn't care if he needs my help or not."

Kelly laid a hand over Melanie's. "But you do."

A sigh slipped from her lips. "Yeah."

"What you have is a conundrum, my friend."

Melanie grinned. "You helping Peter study for his English tests again?" Kelly often used car time with her captive child audience to do test review.

"Hey, it helps dispel my soccer mom image when I throw out a multisyllable word." Kelly winked.

"You'll be ready for *Jeopardy!* before that boy graduates high school." Melanie laughed, then sobered and returned to the subject she'd been avoiding. "I guess the real problem is that I don't want to go to that reunion and tell everyone…" Her voice trailed off. She stirred at her coffee with a spoon, even though it was already fully sugared up. "Well, that I'm not what they expected me to be."

"What? You *didn't* become what you imagined on graduation day?" Kelly clutched at her chest in mock horror. "Who does, Melanie? Heck, most of us have no idea what we want to be when we grow up. And a good chunk of us never do. Take my husband, for instance. He just bought an ATV. *An ATV.* We live in a subdivision, for Pete's sake. Where's he planning on riding it? Around the cul-de-sac?"

Melanie laughed. "I thought he was sold on getting a jet ski."

"Apparently those are a little hard to use on the grass. The man forgets we live on eight acres in *Indiana,* not to mention an hour away from the closest thing to jet ski water." Kelly threw up her hands in a "duh" gesture. "So now he's hell-bent on saving for a lake house. I swear, that man has more toys than our ten-year-old."

Melanie fingered the spoon, then finally let it rest. "At my age, you'd think I'd be well adjusted enough that I wouldn't worry about what people at the class reunion think of me. I mean, I'm a *grown-up*."

Kelly laughed. "Honey, even Miss America worries about what people will think of her at her reunion. I don't know what it is about those things, but they always bring out our inner seventh-grader."

Melanie nodded in agreement, drew in a breath and held tight to the stoneware mug. "Cade said he'll cosign on my loan if I help him at the reunion."

"A little quid pro quo?" Kelly grinned. "Sorry. That was on last week's test." Her gaze softened. "What does Cade want you to help him with?"

"Networking at the reunion. Cade's a master in the courtroom, but put him in the middle of a cocktail party and he's totally out of his element. He gives new meaning to the words social faux pax."

Kelly chuckled, twirling the straw in her frozen mocha. "Do you think he asked you for this favor because he secretly wants to try to get the two of you back together?"

Melanie glanced again at her daughter, and wondered about the glances she'd seen Emmie exchange with Cade. The good mood Emmie had been in this morning had lasted all day, clearly a sign something was up.

Ha, like what *Emmie* was trying to cook up was the problem. Today, Melanie had found herself exchanging a few glances of her own with Cade. The year apart had only seemed to intensify her gut reaction to his presence, as if her hormones had been silently building, waiting for the trigger of Cade to set them off.

Hormones could be kept under control. She wasn't going to let a little desire send her running back into a marital mistake.

"Even if he does," Melanie said, "it's not

going to happen. I can't go back to being the little wife."

"What if that's not what Cade wants? What if he's changed?"

"If there's one thing I know about Cade, it's how much he likes things to stay exactly the same. He loved knowing I'd be there at the end of the day when he came in from work. He liked wearing his blue suit on Mondays, the gray on Tuesdays. Eating spaghetti every Thursday night, like our lives were a stuck record."

"Surely you don't think he wanted that at the expense of your dreams?"

Melanie considered her friend's comment for a moment, sipping her coffee. "I don't think Cade ever set out to hurt me, to purposely stuff me in this little Stepford box. We stepped into these roles and then it got easier to go on playing them, rather than changing the game halfway through. He wanted a wife who would arrange the dinner parties, pack his suitcases, have his dinner waiting. He's a good man, but a stickler for tradition." Melanie rose and deposited her empty mug in the sink, then returned to Kelly, lowering her voice so Emmie wouldn't overhear. "For Cade, sameness is security and we got into one heck of a secure rut. He needs something different from a marriage than I can give. I don't want a man who loves me for my ability to cook a crown roast for twelve. Whether or not he looks good in a suit on the night of the reunion, I'm not falling back into that same trap and letting my emotions override my brain."

Like that hadn't happened a hundred times already today. When Cade was in the shop, Melanie had been intensely aware of his every move. The scent of his cologne, the blue of his eyes, the very nearness of him.

The bell over the door jingled again, the spring breeze whisking in with Ben Reynolds, the owner of the pawn shop next door. An instant smile lit up his friendly features, putting light into his gray eyes. "Hi, Melanie." He took off his fedora and clasped it between his hands.

"Ben! Hi! Can I get you a cup of coffee?"

"No, thanks. I came by to talk to you." He ran his fingers around the rim of the hat. Clearly he wasn't here for his regular daily chitchat and cappuccino. Dread tightened in Melanie's gut.

She told Kelly she'd be back in a second, then led the way to the love seats, vacated earlier by a couple who had lingered there for a few hours.

"I hate to tell you this because I know you wanted my place," Ben said after they were seated, "but I got an offer today."

An offer already? The place wasn't even listed with a realtor yet, though nearly all of

Ben's customers knew he wanted to retire and sell the space. "I'm working on getting the bank loan, Ben, you know that."

"I need to sell as fast as I can. Peggy's mom is getting worse. That heart attack really did a number on her. Peggy wants us to move to Phoenix soon as we can, to help her mom out. Plus, I'm done with Indiana winters. If I never see another shovelful of snow, I can die happy."

"You've been a great friend, Ben," she said, laying a hand on his arm. "You were the first to welcome me to the neighborhood, and the most vocal advertiser for my shop I've ever met. I understand your position. You do what you need to for your family."

Ben's face took on an apologetic cast. "I still feel bad, knowing how much you want the space. If you could find a way to get the funding faster…" He threw up his hands.

"I understand."

Ben gave her a sympathetic smile. "Think about it for a second. I'm going to take you up on that coffee offer." He headed over to the counter and ordered his usual decaf from Emmie.

Melanie watched him walk away and knew there wasn't another way. Melanie had already talked to two banks this past week and she'd heard the same thing—once she had a couple years under her belt, with the business showing a steady profit, they'd be more inclined to lend her the money. Otherwise, without much for assets behind her, she didn't have a chance of getting the money.

Being a housewife and a room mom apparently hadn't given her the kind of solid financial background bankers liked to see.

Until now, she'd run her company on her own terms, without needing to use Cade or her marital status. Everything was in her own name. The start-up expenses had been small enough that she was able to cover the majority of them with an inheritance from her grandmother and the sale of the few remaining antiques in the shop. The rest she'd paid for with credit cards, taking a leap of faith that the market for a coffee shop would be much stronger than that of an aging antiques shop.

The gamble had paid off. Melanie had no debt, and was pleased to finally see more pluses on her balance sheet every month.

With the expansion, she could double her sales. Being located across the street from Lawford University provided a steady under-twenty-five clientele that increased by thirty percent each month. Coupled with the businesspeople who worked in the area and stopped in throughout the day for a caffeine boost, Cuppa Life had a pretty continual customer flow.

Melanie glanced at the door. Cade had left an hour ago, for a meeting with a client. His offer still rang in her head.

That offer came with some strings, but they were strings Melanie was willing to accept, if it meant she could finally have the business she'd envisioned. She could handle this— handle being around Cade—all without losing her heart or her head.

"Ben, don't worry," Melanie said, coming up to the older man just as he was about to put on his hat and head back out the door. "I'll have the funding. Give me two weeks."

The man who had dispensed wonderful business advice in exchange for a free espresso here and there, nodded. "You've got your two weeks, Melanie. But after that...I have to think of my own family. I'm sorry."

"Two weeks," she reiterated. "I'll make it happen."

How hard could it be? She'd attend the reunion next Friday night, help Cade as she always had, just one more time. In the end, it would mean she'd see her dream fulfilled.

All she had to do was pretend she was married to Cade. After nineteen years in the job, she'd perfected the happy wife role.

Too bad her heart was no longer in it.

"You did *what?*"

Cade swung his racket, sending the tennis ball over the net and onto the cushy green court on Carter's side. He was glad for his weekly early Saturday morning tennis match with his twin brother. After all that had happened in Melanie's coffee shop, he needed to expend some energy and frustration. It was either tennis or pounding some walls. Considering his lack of expertise in the handyman arena, this was a better option, particularly for his walls. "I asked Melanie to go to the reunion with me."

Carter lobbed the ball back. "I thought you guys were getting divorced."

"That's the plan." *Maybe.* He smacked the ball over the net.

"Uh-huh. You're thinking you'll get her all dressed up—" Carter let out a grunt as he hit the yellow sphere "—you throw on a tie, take her out on the dance floor a couple of times, waltz around to some Sinatra. Before you know it, you're in love again, just like in high school?"

Cade made an easy return, then shrugged. "Hey, it happens in the movies."

Carter reached high, nicking the ball a moment before it flew past him. "Real life doesn't work like that."

"Why not? Melanie and I were happy for years." Cade waited for the bounce, then returned again.

"Women today expect more."

Cade arched a brow. "Says the man who thinks marriage is a contagious disease."

"At least I know better than to create a business plan to win a woman over. I know you, Cade, you've probably got a ten-point strategic overview all laid out on how to win Melanie's heart. You've analyzed the pros and cons, created a damned spreadsheet for your options and even calculated the odds on flowers versus diamonds."

Cade scowled. "I have not."

Okay, he did have a list. But he didn't have a spreadsheet and certainly hadn't used a calculator to determine the best course of action.

"If you haven't, which I highly doubt, you will." Carter got the serve this time and sent the ball over the net toward his brother. "You're the most uptight man I know. If you weren't my twin brother, I'd think you were an alien."

"Speaking of nonhuman creatures," Cade said, grinning as he slammed the ball back with enough force to tell his brother he was definitely done with the subject of his marriage. "What's new with you?"

"Funny you should ask," Carter said as he waited for the bounce before swinging his racket. "Remember Uncle Neil's will?"

Cade nodded. He'd been at the reading last month. Uncle Neil, a lifelong bachelor, had divvied up his companies and his possessions among his few nephews and nieces. Cade and Melanie had inherited a house in Cape Cod, a nice beach place that he remembered going to as a kid.

Someday, maybe, Melanie would want to go there. More specifically, go there with Cade. Take a weekend, stroll on the sand and rekindle the flame that had seemed to grow smaller since they'd married.

Then again, at the rate his reconciliation efforts were going, he'd be best off selling the place.

"Did you decide what to do with that toy company you inherited?" Cade said.

Carter drew in a breath. "Yep. I quit my job last week and moved into Uncle Neil's office."

"You did?"

"I'm sick of the corporate rat race," Carter said. "I don't know how you've stood it this long."

Cade hadn't. In the last few years, Cade had grown more and more frustrated with his job, with working for his father, and for the first time ever, wondered if he'd made a mistake by following in his father's footsteps. Cade was a good lawyer—but lately not a happy one.

For a second, he envied Carter's ability to chuck it all, take a chance. Pursue a dream that might not work out. Just as Melanie had.

Cade shrugged off the thought. It was probably some early onset midlife crisis. He'd buy a convertible and highlight his hair and be over it.

But as he looked at his twin brother, at the excitement in his eyes as he talked about the toy company between racket swings, Cade had to wonder if he needed more than a few hundred horsepower to erase this feeling.

"Anyway, the company's been struggling for a while," Carter said. "Morale is in the toilet, sea turtles have faster production than I do. I have to do something, but toys aren't quite my strong suit."

"They aren't mine, either," Cade said, sending another serve over the net. "We didn't exactly have a lot of playtime when we were kids."

"Yeah, that being responsible thing kind of kills the opportunity for a little cops and robbers in the backyard."

Cade missed the shot and cursed. He had no desire to revisit his childhood. Once had been enough. It hadn't been happy, it hadn't been fun and no one knew that better than Carter. No need to reopen old wounds.

"Anyway," Carter said, pausing to take a breather, "I was wondering if you knew anyone who specialized in that whole revitalizing a company thing."

"I heard about a firm in Lawford, Creativity Masters. The client I met with, Homesoft Toilet Paper, was singing their praises."

"They found a way to make toilet paper creative?" Carter chuckled, then swung and hit the ball back. "My toy company should be a piece of cake after a few rolls of squeezably soft."

Cade cut off a laugh as he returned the ball with a hard, swift swing. Once again, the feeling that he was missing something returned. Maybe Cade needed a little creativity boost for his own life.

He wondered vaguely what he would have done differently, had he been able to go back to prom night and change the course he and Melanie had taken. Would he have gone into another field? Tried another avenue?

Carter reached to the right, smacked the yellow ball with his racket and let out a curse when it sailed outside of the white lines, bouncing against the fence. He paused, dropping his hands to his knees and inhaling, sweat beading across his brow. "I'm getting my butt beat. Can't you let a man win once in a while? Protect his ego?"

Cade retrieved the ball, then bounced it on the court a couple of times before readying it for serve, giving each of them a breather. "Lay off the doughnuts in the break room and you'll be able to reach those high shots."

"It's not the doughnuts. It's the reception-ist." Carter grinned. "Late night with Deanna. I'm not operating on all cylinders."

"When have you *ever* operated on all your cylinders?"

"That was always your job," Carter said with a grin.

That was true. Cade had shouldered the paternal expectations, gone into the family firm, fulfilled the next generation of Matthews lawyers. Carter, however, had been the one with charm, who smiled his way through college, with job offers falling at his feet like starry-eyed coeds. He'd had options—something Cade had never even considered.

For a moment, Cade envied his twin, the freedom he had to quit the accounting firm for a spin at toy making. Cade shook it off. It was simply a restlessness, maybe brought about from another birthday that edged him closer to forty. He didn't need an escape from his job, he just needed a way to deal with the fact that his perfect life had disintegrated.

Cade slammed the serve over to Carter's side, making him dash to the right and dive to return. "To win back a woman like Melanie," he said, undeterred by the conversation detour, "you're going to need a hell of a lot more than your navy Brooks Brothers and a spray of roses, you know."

"I know how Melanie's mind works." The ball sailed into Carter's side of the court, an inch past the reach of his racket. Carter cursed again.

"I hate to tell you this, Cade," Carter said, lowering his racket and approaching the net, his breath coming in little gasps. "But you're a detail guy. When it comes to women, detail guys have no chance. You need to be a concept man, so you can see the whole picture and fill in the blanks you've missed with her. It's not about red roses over pink, Cade, it's about seeing what's bugging her."

"I was married to Melanie for nineteen years. I know the whole picture." But clearly, he'd missed something behind the canvas.

"If that's so, why is she divorcing you?" Carter gave him a sympathetic glance. All their lives, Carter had been the only one who knew what made Cade tick, and how to get right to the heart of Cade's problems. "Sorry to say it, man, but that's the one fly in your ointment. Until you figure out what's behind her leaving, you'll never be able to convince her to stay."

"So now you're the expert on women?"

"Hey, I never said I knew how to keep one." Carter grinned, the same grin that had stolen—and broken—dozens of female hearts. "Just how to get one."

Five minutes later, they called the game a draw. As Cade retrieved the tennis ball and headed toward the locker room with Carter, he knew his twin brother was right. Whatever had caused Melanie to leave was still there, the eight-hundred-pound relationship gorilla in the room.

If his twin could chuck his career and go into toy making, then maybe Cade could untangle the yo-yo string around his heart.

He was, as Carter said, a detail guy. If he could find the one detail he'd overlooked, then maybe he could restore the life he'd had.

And if not, there was always Chicago.

CHAPTER FIVE

MELANIE STARED AT THE reflection in the mirror. She'd have to be a magician to make this work.

There was no way she could pull off eighteen again. She wasn't sure she could even pull off thirty-seven, not with those crow's feet and hips.

"I'm insane for doing this," she told Kelly, who had volunteered to go dress shopping with her on Saturday morning. Emmie was running the shop, Kelly's kids were at a sleep-over party for a cousin, leaving the two free to enjoy a rare couple of hours in the mall. Well, enjoying wasn't exactly the word, considering Melanie was in a dressing room standing in a front of a three-way mirror that made painfully clear the effects of one too many mocha lattes.

"That's a great dress," Kelly said, standing behind Melanie. "It's got a lot of va-va-voom." For emphasis, she gave her hips a little shimmy.

"I don't need va-va-voom for a class reunion." Melanie pivoted to go back into the dressing room, take the dress off and go for something more in her usual style—meaning something totally *un*-voomed.

Before she could, Kelly caught her by the shoulders and turned her back to the mirror, waiting while Melanie took in the image of the dress. "Look at yourself," she said softly.

Melanie did, shaking off the doubts of a nearly forty-year-old woman, and gave herself a second, less jaded look. The deep maroon fabric hugged along her curves, slipping down her hips before flaring out in a flirty skirt that begged for twirling. The halter top had a deep V neckline and a nice amount of side support, giving Melanie the illusion of far more cleavage than she really had. It was sexy, glamorous, the kind of dress worn by women ten years younger, a hundred times more sophisticated.

Women other than her.

"You look positively gorgeous," Kelly said. "If I had a figure like that after having my two, I'd be celebrating it, not hiding it." She stepped back and indicated Melanie's reflection again. "And whether you do it for Cade or just to make jaws drop, you should buy this dress."

"I'm a jeans and T-shirt kind of girl. I should wear one of the dresses I wore to Cade's lawyer functions." Melanie stepped back, smoothed a hand down the slippery fabric. "Except those are…well, dowdy. Mom and wife stuff. You don't do va-va-voom at a client dinner."

"Yeah, and that hardworking mom and business owner look is all the rage at reunions this year." Kelly slipped around Melanie to come between her and her reflection. "If you want different results for your life, you have to stop doing—and wearing—the same old thing."

"But—"

"Don't you but me. You know you've done that with everything else—your marriage, your business—everything *but* yourself." Kelly gave her an understanding smile. "We're in the same club, you and I. We sign up for it in that first Lamaze class. It's the Put Yourself Last club, after the guy, after the kid, heck, I'm even after the dog. It's time for you to let Melanie shine. And that dress," Kelly said, "is going to shine so much, you're going to blind everyone." She grinned, then moved away and waved a hand toward the mirror.

This time, Melanie looked with objective

eyes, seeing herself as Kelly did, pushing away the thoughts that she was too old, too conservative…too everything for this dress.

A smile curved across her face. "It does look good, doesn't it?" She spun to one side, then the other, watching the skirt twirl against her legs.

"I'd lose the white ankle socks, though."

Melanie laughed at her footwear staple. "I promise."

She stayed there a moment longer, slipping into the habit of envisioning Cade's reaction to her appearance. How he'd smile at the way the dress flattered the parts of her body he most admired.

Like her legs, her breasts. Heck, he'd been happy with about anything, back in those early years, before the sizzle in their marriage had gone from full boil to simmer before finally dissolving.

A memory of him, coming into the

bedroom while she was getting ready for a rare evening out—their fifteenth anniversary—sprang to mind. Melanie, in high heels and a little black dress, busy fastening the diamond earrings he'd given her onto her ears, hadn't heard him come in. He'd snuck up from behind, stealing his arms around her waist, pressing a kiss to her neck, then turning her slowly, oh so slowly, in his arms, until her lips were beneath his—

And they ended up twenty minutes late for their dinner reservations.

If she wore this on Friday night, would Cade do that again? Would he kiss her like he used to, erasing the past year, closing the ever-widening gap between them?

Would he once again make her feel like the only woman in the world? She closed her eyes, bittersweet longing washing over her.

"I'll get the dress," Melanie said, still

wrapped up in the luxurious feel of the silky fabric against her legs, the memories of Cade.

"Good. Now let's go pick out my favorite part." Kelly's eyes glistened with excitement. "The shoes."

A few minutes later, Melanie and Kelly left the mall, a little lighter in their wallets. Melanie swung her new dress over her shoulder, matching heels dangling from a bag attached to the hanger.

Kelly held up the bag containing two new pairs of sexy summer sandals. "When it comes to shoes, I might as well just hand over my credit card the second I walk into the department. I never leave empty-handed."

Melanie laughed. "I'm that way with coffee cups. I have a whole collection of them on the back wall of the shop. Some of them are antiques, some just caught my eye in a store."

Her friend shook her head. "You are *so* not normal."

Melanie laughed again. "Thanks for dragging me out of Cuppa Life to go shopping. I needed this."

"As long as you promise to run interference when Roger sees the Visa bill."

"All you have to do is wear a sexy little dress and he'll forget all about it." As the words left Melanie's mouth, however, she realized she'd never really done that with Cade.

Except for those rare special occasions, she'd never donned a sexy dress just to see him smile, or distract him from his day. From the start, their marriage had been wrapped around Emmie, and struggling to survive on the minimal income they'd made while Cade worked his way through law school and then up the firm's ladder. Melanie had worn the uniform of a mom—sweats, no makeup and hair in a ponytail.

Then, as Emmie grew up and Cade grew busier at work, the number of hours in a day seemed to shorten and the distance between her and her husband had seemed to lengthen, regardless of whether she remembered to put on a little mascara and lip gloss. The problems that they had went unresolved, pushed to the side. After too many years of ignoring the issues, those problems had become too big, too complicated to solve with a little black dress.

What had she been thinking? That a dress would somehow magically erase the illusions she'd had about their marriage? That wouldn't happen, no matter how much she might wish it. Melanie had to be realistic, not get wrapped up in a silky fabric and a handful of memories that stubbornly lingered.

In the parking lot, Melanie hugged Kelly and said goodbye, then slipped into her own car and headed back to Cuppa Life, resolved to put Cade from her mind for the rest of the day.

"Hey, Mom! What'd you get?" Emmie handed Cooter his regular blend, stamped his frequent visitor card, then turned to face Melanie as she came around the counter.

"A dress." Melanie slipped on an apron, then whisked her hair up into a ponytail. Back to regular ol' Melanie.

"I know that." Emmie rolled her eyes. "Details, Mom. I need details."

"Well, it's knee-length, a kind of burgundy-pink and…" She paused, avoiding Emmie's inquisitive gaze by busying herself with washing her hands.

Emmie put a fist on her hip. "And what?"

"Well, it's a little sexy."

"Way to go, Mom." Emmie let out a low

whistle. "I never would have pegged *you* for a sexy dress."

"Hey, I was sexy once." Put that way, it sounded pretty darn pitiful. When she'd been Emmie's age, she'd worried about her appearance, spending hours in the mall, poring over fashion magazines, and then trying one outfit after another until she had the perfect one. Since she'd gotten married, she hadn't let herself go—exactly—she'd simply had other priorities to take up her days. Priorities that didn't include makeup, curling irons and especially didn't include sexy dresses.

She thought back to the image of herself in the mirror, the way the skirt swirled around her legs, how every inch of the maroon fabric had accentuated curves lost behind her Cuppa Life apron. Maybe it was time to revamp that priority list.

After all, she was thirty-seven, not dead.

"I bet Dad will love what you bought." Emmie threw the words out as casually as bread crumbs.

Melanie started restocking the small under-the-counter refrigerator with milk and cream. "I'm not wearing it for him."

Liar, her mind whispered. She was, too. Because a part of her still craved his sexy smile, that light in his eyes when he looked at her.

"Uh-huh," Emmie said.

Melanie brushed the thoughts away. Thinking about Cade's reactions would only send her back down the very road she'd left last year. A road Emmie seemed to be ignoring lately, as if she saw the separation as a phase her parents were going through.

"Emmie," Melanie said softly, laying a hand on her daughter's. "Dad and I *are* getting divorced. Please don't read anything into a dress."

Emmie scowled. "You guys are always telling me not to give up, to keep going for what I want. Why is it okay for you to do it?"

"I'm not giving up."

"What do you call a divorce? Why don't you two just sit down and talk?"

"We have, sweetheart." But a little voice inside asked if she'd simply taken the easier road.

"Maybe you didn't try hard enough." Emmie's words were sharp with anger.

Melanie sighed. "It's more complicated than trying harder. Than a conversation."

Emmie threw up her hands. "I am so sick of this, of going to your apartment, then Dad's house, and seeing both of you totally miserable. You've always told me relationships take work. Well, why don't you two practice what you preach?" She stalked off to the rest room, ignoring Melanie's calls for her to come back.

Melanie rubbed at the knot of tension in the back of her neck. Emmie didn't know the whole story. And there was no way Melanie was going to fill in the details Emmie was missing. Melanie closed her eyes and those very details came flooding back, ending with that day in the hospital. She'd been scared, crying and alone.

Always alone. Because when it came to priorities, Cade's had always been work.

Emmie's youthful idealization of the situation made her see it in simple black and white terms. Melanie knew there was far too much gray to sort things out. Even if for a little while today, she'd thought maybe—

Maybe they could.

"You got a real firecracker there," Cooter said, raising his coffee in the direction Emmie had gone.

Melanie smiled politely. "Yeah."

"You know, your man trouble reminds me of a story." Cooter rose and crossed to the one of the bar stools. He ran his hand down the length of his white beard, gearing up.

"Cooter, I—"

"There's these two old women, real biddies, the kind who sit in the sun and yak the day away." Cooter looked to Melanie, waiting for her to nod in understanding. "One of 'em, she's got this dog and it's moaning. The other says, 'What's wrong with your dog?' The first lady looks at the idiot of a pooch and says, 'He's been eatin' wood chips. Tears up his belly somethin' fierce.' Second lady shakes her head. 'Why would he do that, if it hurts?' First lady throws up her hands. 'I dunno. Guess he ain't gotten smart enough yet to quit.'" Cooter grinned at her, as if he'd just given her the secret to life.

"That's a…great story," Melanie said. "I think."

"It means," Cooter said, leaning forward, his light blue eyes bright, "you keep doin' stupid things until they hurt you enough and then you get smart enough to quit." He gave her a nod, then returned to his coffee and his paper.

Melanie shook her head. Cooter had a habit of dispensing wisdom wrapped in allegories. She wasn't quite sure if his tidbit today was about her relationship with Emmie—or with Cade. Or heck, the hot plate she'd burned her thumb on earlier today.

The door jingled and Melanie turned, expecting the next influx of college students. Instead Cade stood in the doorway, still dressed in his suit—his fighting clothes, he used to call them—but a little more rumpled than when he'd started his day. His dark blue tie was loosened at the neck of his white button-down shirt, giving him an air of vulnerability. He looked like a little boy trying to escape the confines of his Sunday best.

Then Cade strode forward, with the same comfortable, assured step he'd always had, and any comparisons to preschoolers ended.

Her stomach flipped over, heavy with a desire that she'd thought had long ago disappeared. But no, it was there, just waiting for Cade. His smile. His touch.

"Hi, Melanie."

Two words and everything within her shuddered to a stop. Damn Cade for still having that power over her. A year apart and a simple glance could still awaken the spark that had first drawn her to him.

A spark, however, wasn't enough to rebuild—and maintain—the fire they'd needed as adults. If it had, it would have gotten them through the roughest parts, the days when one needed the other, and that call had gone unanswered.

"Do you want some coffee?" Melanie said, getting to her feet and putting the counter's width between them.

"Sure." He slid onto one of the bar stools. His face was lined with exhaustion. Melanie's hand ached to reach out, to touch him and wipe all that away. Despite everything they'd gone through, she still worried about him. Some feelings, she'd found, couldn't be turned off like a dripping garden hose.

Either way, Cade wouldn't want her to do that. If there was one thing Cade prided himself on, it was his "can do no matter what" attitude. If only he'd relied on her more, talked more.

She slid a cup of black Kenyan roast across the counter, knowing from all their years together that he wouldn't want anything fancier. "Here you go. On the house."

"Thanks."

"So…" she began, after he took a long sip but still didn't speak, "why did you stop in today?" He'd been here twice in the space of two days, after nearly a year of separation that hadn't involved more than a couple of quick run-ins at events for Emmie. There had to be a reason—Cade Matthews was a man who didn't waste time, or make a half-hour journey if he didn't have an agenda.

He cupped his hands around the mug, staring at the coffee for a long second before looking up and meeting Melanie's gaze. "Are you happy here?"

"Yes," she answered, no reservations in her voice. "I love working for myself."

"Good."

He didn't go on and Melanie told herself not to push. But then she found her mouth opening anyway, out of habit, out of something more, she didn't know. "What's bothering you, Cade?"

He drew in a breath, then slid the coffee to the side. "I don't know. Maybe I've just been putting in too many hours lately. Or had too many frustrating clients."

"You're not enjoying your job anymore?" she asked, surprised. There'd never been a day where she'd seen Cade anything but charged to get to the office. Perhaps that was why he was interviewing with Bill, to find a new challenge. Or maybe he'd finally grown tired of being under his father's demanding rule.

"I have a trial next month," he went on. "Trademark infringement. One of those really big battles. On any other day, I'd be charged up, ready to hit it head-on."

"But not today?"

He shrugged. "It's like I've already been

there, done that. I don't know…maybe I'm just looking for something different."

Cade unsure? Questioning his job? Either he was an alien replacement of his former self or—

There was no "or." The Cade she knew hadn't had a day of indecision. Perhaps he felt out of sorts now that the divorce was becoming a reality.

"I stopped by because I had an idea. An idea for you and me," he said, putting up a hand. "Don't say no until you've heard me out."

"Okay…" She leaned back against the small refrigerator and crossed her arms over her chest. The appliance hummed against her back.

"We've been apart for a year and if we go to the reunion as we are now, I'm sure that's going to show."

"Oh, I don't—"

"It will, Melanie. We're not close like we used to be."

"We were never close, Cade." The harsh truth sat there between them, heavy and immovable. She'd thought they were, once, but it had disappeared, lost in Cade's relentless work schedule and her busy days of being room mom and child chauffeur.

In the dark of night, she longed for that closeness again. Longed for Cade, for the days when he'd crawled into bed and wrapped his arms around her, making it seem as if anything in the world was possible. Then work had taken him away more and more—physically, emotionally—and those times had stopped.

"Either way," Cade continued, "I don't want to walk into that room and let the entire senior class know we're having problems."

Those *would* show, without a doubt. The old Cade and Melanie had been glued at the hip, always touching or flirting, and making so many public displays of affection, PDAs, as Emmie called them, that anyone within a five-county radius could tell they were in love. "Since when did you start worrying about what other people think?"

His eyes met hers and in them, she saw much more than exhaustion. Loneliness. Regret. But then he swallowed, and it all disappeared, replaced with Can-Do Cade. Disappointment flickered inside her. "I don't. I just want this to be convincing for Bill."

She slapped a smile on her face. "Of course." The career, always the career. If anything told her Cade hadn't changed, it was that sentence.

"In order to do that, I think we need to spend a little time together."

Time with Cade? That couldn't be good. Judging by the way her hormones were scrambling a counterattack to her common sense, she knew spending more time with him would only give the estrogen a little more am-munition. "Do you mean dating?" she said, nearly knocking over the sugar as she moved away from him and the idea. "Because I don't think that's a good idea."

"Why not?"

She sighed. Why did he have to be so obtuse about this? Wasn't the moving out, the serving of papers, the year apart, all one huge bullhorn announcing that it was over? "We're getting a divorce, Cade. Please don't make it any harder than it already is."

"Is it hard on you, Melanie?" His gaze locked on hers, the deep blue eyes she'd stared into for more than half her life missing nothing, and displaying frustration and hurt. "Because it sure doesn't seem it."

"Of course it is." She turned away, ignoring the sudden burning behind her eyes. Did he think she'd left their marriage impetuously? That any of this had been an easy decision?

She busied herself with wiping an already clean counter, instead of dwelling on the what-ifs and the storm whipped up by Cade's presence.

When she glanced at him again, he seemed to have tamped down the temporary flare of emotion. As always, Cade was back to being cool, calm and collected. Never betray a weakness, he'd always told her, particularly in a courtroom.

And he never had. Especially with her. And especially not when it had mattered.

If he had…

But he hadn't.

"Anyway," Cade said, clearing his throat, "I thought maybe I could work here for a few days. From what Emmie says, this place is busier than a zoo, and you could use the help. She said the student you had working here quit last week." He grinned, and her heart—which had never done a good job of listening to her mind—skipped a beat. "Plus, I'll work for free."

"Work here?" She paused, the sponge dripping onto her toes. Had she heard him right? "Why would you want to do that?"

"I told you. We need to spend some time together. It seems like a win-win to me."

Melanie eyed the man she had lived with for all of her adult years and knew he was hiding something. It wasn't just about putting on a good show for Bill Hendrickson at the reunion.

She had to wonder if Cade's win-win also involved winning her heart again. As much as a part of her—the lonely part that shared a bed with extra pillows instead of a husband—might wish otherwise, Melanie knew that was the one thing not up for grabs.

CHAPTER SIX

"I'M INSANE," Melanie said to Kelly the next morning. They were alone in the shop, something that wouldn't last long on a Sunday. Soon as church services were over, the shop would pick up again. The college kids wouldn't be here until they rolled out of bed and came in for a little caffeine to counteract the frat party headache, but after that, business would be pretty steady until late afternoon. "Why did I ever agree to let Cade work here? I'm trying to divorce him, not hire him."

Kelly ran a finger along the rim of her coffee mug. "Maybe a tiny part of you doesn't want to divorce him."

Melanie shook her head, resolute. "This is the best thing, trust me. Cade isn't going to change."

Hadn't he proved that yesterday? Just when she thought he might be a little vulnerable, might tell her some of the secrets he kept locked in his heart—

He'd mentioned work. Always the job, never the man, never how he felt.

"Whatever you say." Kelly shrugged, but there was disbelief in her face. "He's your husband."

"Not anymore."

As the words left her, though, they were tinged with sadness. What would her life ahead be like without Cade? She'd been so busy getting the business off the ground that she hadn't paused to dwell on the empty rooms of her apartment, the lack of a second voice at home.

How would it be to wake up in five years, ten, and realize Cade was truly gone from her life? That the man she'd spent half her life loving was with someone else? Melanie shook the thoughts off. A bit of regret was normal with any divorce, no matter how the marriage had ended. After all, she'd been with Cade for twenty years. She'd only dated two other guys before him. He was what she knew, what she'd always known, and giving that up for good was bound to leave her a little melancholy.

Add to that seeing him again after a year apart and Melanie had a Betty Crocker-worthy recipe for regret. That's all it was—the opposite of cold feet. Regardless of what she might think she saw in his eyes or felt in her chest, she wasn't going to change her mind. The decision had been hard enough to make—there would be no rethinking of it.

"So, when's he coming in?" Kelly asked.

Melanie glanced at the clock, watching the

hand sweep upward to nine o'clock. "Any minute now. I thought he could learn the ropes today. The weekdays are way too busy for me to have time to show him anything."

"Sure you don't want me to stay?"

Melanie grinned. "You're just looking for an excuse to get out of that baby shower."

"Hey, I am so done with diapers, I don't even want to look at them. Even the smell of rash cream brings back bad memories." Kelly rose, pushing her empty cup to the side. She laughed. "Oh, what am I saying? I miss my boys being little. Every time I turn around, they've grown six inches." She let out a sigh, then swung her purse over her shoulder. "Maybe I'll take a sniff of the Desitin. Just for old times' sake."

Melanie was still laughing after Kelly had left, a second morning brew in a to-go cup. Five seconds later, the bell jingled and Cade walked in, wearing jeans and a blue T-shirt. Emblazoned across his chest was an ad for a wine festival.

Cade.

She watched him cross the room, still handsome as any man she'd ever seen in a magazine, with that lazy, tempting grin and a twinkle in his eyes that seemed to always tease at the edges of laughter. She told herself he no longer affected her. That she could get through a day of working with him—

And not lose her mind or worse, her heart.

Yet, as he drew closer and she read the words curving across his chest, her heart stopped with the memory of the fall weekend when they'd driven up to Michigan to attend the wine festival. Two, no, three years ago. She'd planned the time away for a couple of weeks, reminding Cade several times to clear the weekend on his schedule.

She'd rented a room at a bed-and-breakfast, bought a little sexy black nothing, and hoped the two days alone would bring back the magic that seemed to have disappeared sometime between late night bottle feedings and school plays. She'd thought it would be as simple as throwing on a lacy negligee and spending a few extra hours in bed.

It hadn't. The weekend had been a disaster of epic proportions, with Cade talking on his cell phone more than to his wife. There'd been one moment, when they'd spread out a blanket on the grass, shared a bottle of Chardonnay and a block of cheese, and laughed—oh, how they'd laughed. She'd thought maybe…just maybe, they were re-capturing the magic.

Then his phone had rung and the spell had shattered as easily as a crystal vase dropped on concrete.

And yet, as Cade approached, Melanie found herself wondering if that spell had really been broken or merely needed to be reworked a bit.

"So," Cade said, "where do you want me? I'm dressed to work."

Cade had taken her "dress casual" advice to heart and was clearly attempting to appear relaxed. Between the Levi's and the way he was leaning on the counter, he was the poster boy for relaxed. Only she knew that underneath that well-pressed T lurked a man who hated any kind of disorder.

Nevertheless, desire stirred within her, picturing them together again. On the counter. Against the wall. In her bed. She ran a hand over hot cheeks and pushed the fantasy away.

"How about we start with the basics?" Melanie said, keeping her focus on work, not the shirt and the memories it resurrected. And certainly not on Cade's face, on eyes that still had the power to set her pulse off-kilter. "I'll show you how to brew the coffee, then we'll work up to cappuccino."

"Before you know it, I'll be a brewmaster." He cocked a grin at her and she found herself returning the smile. He slipped behind the counter to stand next to her. A year ago, when Melanie had opened the shop, the space had seemed so much wider, particularly when it was just her and Emmie. But Cade made the place seem confined, too tight for two.

Or too tight for her and the one man she didn't want to get close to, not again. Too close and she was risking another heartbreak. One was enough.

"Here's our, ah, main coffee station," Melanie said, clearing her throat and indicating a cranberry and black countertop machine with several spouts and dials. "We brew it here, put it in the carafes, then make a fresh pot whenever the coffee's temperature drops below 150 degrees."

"Doesn't that waste a lot of coffee?"

"Not really. On a busy day, we can go through twenty pots or more."

"Can't you use the old coffee to make those iced things?"

"No, not unless you want to risk cross-contamination. For iced coffee, I have a special five-gallon brewing pot." She opened the fridge and indicated a big white plastic container shaped like a coffee urn.

"Do you roast the beans yourself, too?"

She stepped back, surprised. "You've been reading."

He gave her a grin as familiar as her own palm. "You know me. I always do my homework."

Except for with me, she wanted to add, but

didn't. Cade, who put thought into every decision from the brand of toothpaste he used to the car he drove, hadn't quite applied those same principles when it came to that night twenty years ago in the back of his car.

Heck, neither had she. In those days, they'd thought of nothing but each other. Nothing but the feel of his mouth on hers, his hands on her body, and the sweet release from the thunderstorm continually brewing between them.

"Uh, no, we don't roast our own beans," Melanie said, returning her mind to the subject at hand. "I'd like to get a roaster, but I don't have the room for it."

"Unless you buy the space next door."

"Right." Melanie turned away from Cade's intent gaze and reached for one of the bags of coffee beans, imported from Columbia. "We grind the beans in—"

"Here?" Cade asked, reaching for the grinder at the same time as she did. Their hands collided, sending a rocket propelled grenade of attraction through Melanie. It was a hundred times more intense, a thousand times hotter, than anything she could remember with Cade, as if the time apart had intensified his appeal.

Sexual appeal, she reminded herself. Not marital appeal.

And yet, she didn't pull her hand back right away. She looked up and their gazes met, held. Want tightened its grip on her, holding her captive to the spot. To Cade.

"Melanie," Cade said in the same soft way he used to, as if they were lying together in the dark, not standing in a brightly lit coffee shop on a Sunday morning.

Oh, how I miss him, she thought, the arrow of that lonely, disappointed pain piercing through her. She missed the Cade he used to be, the marriage she had dreamed of having.

Then he leaned down, slow, tentative, his gaze never leaving hers. The heat between them multiplied ten times over with anticipation. With a craving that had never died, despite the year apart.

Kiss me. Her mind willed him to read the unspoken words, to hear the message throbbing in her veins.

He reached for her chin, his large hand cupping her jaw. A tender touch, filled with all the things that Cade never said. "Melanie, I—"

Suddenly she couldn't hear him talk about work. Couldn't bear to hear him disappoint her, to shatter her fantasy that someday, Cade would put her—and their marriage—at the top of the list.

Melanie jerked away, then pushed the

button on the grinder, pulverizing a lot of innocent coffee beans. "This, ah…" Her mind went blank.

"Grinder?" Cade supplied, withdrawing and giving her a knowing smile.

"Yes, thank you." Melanie shifted to business mode. *Treat him like a customer. Treat him like anyone other than the man you pledged to love forever.* "This grinder will take the beans down to grounds in less than thirty seconds. Grind them too long and the grounds become dust. Too short and they're chunky. Grind size can really affect the finished product, so you want this setting right here," she said, pointing at a number on the grinder's dial, "and then the beans are the perfect size for the filter."

Yet, even as she explained the pros and cons of different grind sizes, she was aware of Cade. A few inches away, close enough to touch, should she have that desire.

Heck, she *had* that desire. Always had it. She simply knew better now than to let her hormones make all the decisions.

Twenty minutes later, Cade was brewing his first latte. He'd picked up the intricacies of coffeemaking quickly, as she'd expected. He was a smart man, one who paid attention to the details.

It was the big picture he so often missed.

"You did great," Melanie said, taking a sip of the small latte breve he'd made. "And you added caramel," she said with a smile, noting the flavors that slipped across her taste buds.

"If I remember right, it's your favorite flavor."

"Cade," Melanie began, intending to tell him to stop trying. Her mind was made up, and there would be no undoing the divorce. Regardless of what might happen in one day, or one night, she had nineteen years of mistakes to look back on. Leopards didn't change their spots and career-driven husbands didn't change into family men.

The bell rang, ushering in the first slew of customers. Before she could finish the sentence, she and Cade were busy filling orders and dispensing caffeine. For his first day, he kept up surprisingly well, only looking to her for help a couple of times on a complicated order.

She and Cade slipped into a rhythm, maneuvering around each other in the tight space with ease. If she hadn't known better, she'd have thought Cade had been here forever.

"You did great," Melanie said after the last customers had been served and the door stopped opening. The sun was beginning its late afternoon descent, telling her it was nearly closing time.

"Thanks." He leaned back against the counter and took a long drink of ice water.

"I'm not used to moving so much, though. Guess all those years behind a desk are catching up to me."

Cade was still trim, a man who worked out three mornings a week, rising at four to fit in a trip to the gym before work. He'd kept the same routine all of their married life, jogging in those early days when they couldn't afford a gym membership. She bit her lip instead of telling him he looked as refreshed as the minute he'd stepped in the shop today, as he had the day she'd met him. As sexy as the day he'd told her he loved her. The day he'd asked her to marry him.

"How long until the next rush?"

Melanie glanced at her watch and for a second couldn't read the numbers. She re-doubled her focus. "Anytime now. It won't be long before the study groups and coffee dates head in."

"I never thought this would be such a busy place," he said.

"Yeah." Melanie didn't add anything more. There was no sense in reopening an old wound.

"I'm sorry," he said. "I should have supported you when you said you wanted to open this place."

Melanie stared at Cade, stunned into silence. The man who rarely admitted fault, had just apologized? And over the last straw, the one that had made Melanie finally realize she was being suffocated by her marriage?

Enough avoiding the subject, Melanie decided. "Are you trying to convince me we should get back together? Is that why you're working here? Why you apologized?"

He gave her a grin she could have drawn in her sleep. "Would that be so bad?"

"Yes, Cade, it would be." She lowered her voice, then waited until the final customer had left the shop before continuing. "It's over between us. Don't read anything into this—" she gestured toward him and the coffeemaking "—or my attending the reunion. We made a deal, plain and simple."

"That's all it is? A deal?" He took a step closer, invading her space, once again making her nerves hypersensitive. "Nothing more, Mellie? If so, then I have a deal for you. A very different kind of deal."

Heat and desire wrapped around his words, awakening senses that had been tamped down for so long. *Kiss him,* her body urged. *Kiss him.*

She wanted to, oh how she wanted to. She wanted to pretend the words had never been said, the hurts never inflicted, and that she and Cade could go back to that fairy tale from high school.

She reached out a hand, craving the feel of his cheek beneath her palm, the hard line of his jaw softened by freshly shaven skin. She inhaled, and with that breath, brought in the scent of Cade, a mixture of woods and mint, the same scents that had filled their shared bathroom for a thousand mornings.

She turned away, and started prattling on about the difference between a cappuccino and a latte. If she talked long enough, maybe her mouth could overrun the pounding drumbeat in her pulse.

Drums pounded in his head, an insistent rhythm of want, beating along with the soft jazz coming from the sound system. For a second, Cade thought he had read the same need in Melanie's eyes.

If he bent down and kissed her, would she respond in kind? Melt into his arms, her lips soft and sweet beneath his?

Before he could find out, she'd turned away

and started a coffee demonstration that Cade didn't hear. Every sense had been attuned to her, and it was a long time until his brain stopped picturing her in his arms and his bed.

Cade had what he wanted—an uninterrupted block of time with Melanie. Now he just had to figure out what the hell to do with it.

He'd already screwed up his marriage once—he wasn't one of those men who planted blame squarely on the wife, there had definitely been moments when he hadn't been the best husband—and he had no intentions of doing it a second time, assuming he could figure out what he'd done wrong.

As he listened to her run down a laundry list of ingredients for a Frazzle, his mind reached back over the past years, but he didn't find one place he could point to as the fault line. Sure, there'd been arguments. Moments when neither of them was especially happy, but no one event that glared back at him, an arrow pointing to the big mistake, saying "fix me and all will be as it was."

His marriage had dissolved gradually, like threads in a blanket that came undone a little more each time you placed it on your lap. At night, he paced the living room of the house where he and Melanie had once lived—happily, he'd thought—and found no clues in the beige wall-to-wall carpet and soft sage walls.

He'd played that mental game a thousand times since she'd left and never come any closer to finding the solution than wondering if maybe he'd worked too much, been too un-available to her. He was willing to be avail-able now—and had told her so that night she left—but Melanie had still shut the door and drove away.

Even now, she was shutting him out, except this time she had a cappuccino machine between them, as if holding him at bay with a little steam.

They worked together for a few more hours, the day passing quickly. Before he knew it, Melanie was locking the door and counting the money in the cash register. "We're done already?" he asked.

She nodded. "I close early on Sundays. There's not enough business to justify staying open as late today as I do on the weeknights. During the week, we have the business people and the college students, but on the weekends, the businesses are closed and the students are more often out on dates than here."

Cade glanced at his watch. "It's early." He paused, then figured he needed to bite this bullet someday. "Are the students the only ones with a date?"

"Me?" she looked surprised, then laughed.

"No. I wouldn't have the time or the energy even if someone had asked me out."

No man had asked her out. She was spending her nights alone. Cade figured all the men in Lawford had to be either blind or brain dead to not want Melanie.

"Then how about dinner?" he asked, the words leaving his lips before he could think about the wisdom of the question. "With me."

"Oh, Cade, I really don't think—"

"It's dinner, Melanie. Two chairs, a table and a meal. No hidden strings. No innuendo."

Exhaustion had shaded the area below her eyes. No wonder, too, given the hyperspeed she worked at. He wanted to scoop her up, take her home and tuck her into their queen-size bed, letting her sleep until those shadows disappeared and the smile on her face became brighter, more like the Melanie he used to know.

"You need to eat," he said softly.

"No, I need to get home."

"To what?" Cade took a step closer. "To an empty house? An empty fridge?" Two things he was far too familiar with. "Have dinner with me, Melanie, for old times' sake. Not because you're my wife or because it might lead to something else. Hell, just go because you're hungry and I'm offering a free steak."

"Cade, we're getting—"

"You don't need to remind me every five minutes of the divorce," he said, lashing out, unable to hear that word one more time today. "I know where we're heading. I may not like it, but I've accepted the inevitable."

She took a step closer, her chin upturned, her green eyes afire. "Have you?"

Hell no, he hadn't, but he wasn't going to say it. Instead he let his gaze sweep over her, reading in her eyes the same riot of emotions as earlier. He moved closer to her, coming within inches of her lips. Want curled around his heart, humming within him the familiar song of Melanie, of how she would feel, taste. "Have *you?*"

"Of course I have."

"Then prove it," Cade said, lowering his head, his breath whispering across her lips. "And kiss me."

CHAPTER SEVEN

WHEN CADE KISSED HER, everything within Melanie went from ice-blue to red-hot. It was as if he'd never kissed her before, as if she'd waited for this touch for a lifetime.

With a clarity that astounded her, Melanie remembered every detail of that first, electric touch from twenty years ago, how she'd wanted him all night, fantasizing about the moment when he would finally go beyond holding her hand.

They'd gone to the mall, wandering the tiled space, not buying anything. They'd talked and laughed, all the while aware of the tightening tension between them. When they'd stopped to throw a penny into the fountain, Cade had moved into place behind her, ostensibly to guide her hand, but more, she knew with that instinct every woman possessed, to touch her.

She'd tossed the penny, made the wish that had simmered inside her all night, then turned to him, hoping. As if he'd heard her thoughts, he'd kissed her, under the pale white cast of the lights above them. It had been everything she'd dreamed about—and more. Cade Matthews hadn't disappointed her with his touch.

Not then, and not now.

Those memories washed over her, whispering against this new kiss. Desire arched within her, rumbling through a body that had been focused on business matters for far too long. His lips were tender against hers, drifting over her mouth, an easy, sweet taste of what was to come. Then, when she didn't pull away, his kiss deepened, taking her down a sensuous path so familiar, it nearly made her cry.

She'd missed him, damn it. Missed his kisses, missed his touch. Before she could stop herself, her arms stole around his neck, feeling the ends of his short hair tickle against her skin, making every inch of her want him with a fierceness that bordered on frenzy.

His tongue slipped between her lips and every resolve she'd had melted in the seductive waltz he played on her mouth. She did the same to him, nerve endings tingling with awareness and memory, one fire stoking the other.

He reached up and cupped her jaw, tenderly, in the way he used to, back when their focus had been on each other and nothing else. Behind her closed eyes, a slideshow of memories flashed through Melanie's mind, teasing at the edges of their kiss, urging her to forget the divorce, forget the hurts.

How she wanted to give in to that kiss, to do nothing more than love this man. To let his touch erase the words, the silences, the nights spent alone.

But she had spent too many regretful mornings knowing no kiss could do that.

Melanie jerked back and broke the connection, ignoring the pull of regret. "Cade, we can't do this."

"Why not?" he asked, his gaze still locked on hers. "We're still married."

She turned away, busying herself with cleaning the counter, trying to tamp down the need still rolling inside her. It had been a long, lonely year but she knew she was doing what was best for her, and in the end, for Cade.

"Don't do this, Cade. I can't…" Her voice trailed off, unable to voice the vulnerability still lingering in her chest. If he touched her again, she'd surely dissolve.

"I need you, Melanie," he said, his voice hoarse. "I've always needed you."

"No, you don't. You never did."

He cupped her jaw, tipping her chin upward, waiting for her to meet his gaze. "Melanie, I'd never be where I was today if it wasn't for you. You were always the better half of my success. Of everything."

She shook her head, causing his touch to drop away. "Cade, all I did was bake the leg of lamb and set the table for the dinner parties."

"It was much more than that and you know it."

"Was it? Because I never felt that way. I put on the parties, smiled until my lips hurt, served coffee, tea and your best qualities to every guest. At the end of the night, you were toasting another success and I was washing the damned dishes." She put up a finger when he started to protest. "You forgot me, Cade. Left me behind as you hurried ahead in your career.

The only time you needed me was when there was a party to host or a client to impress."

"I never meant to do that."

She drew in a breath, cooling her temper. "I know, Cade. I guess I just wanted to feel like something I did, something other than raising Emmie, meant something. I never felt that when I was pulling a roast out of the oven or pouring champagne." She glanced around the coffee shop. "Until now."

"What you did mattered, to me," he said.

"You never said it." She let out a little laugh. "Heck, you were never home long enough to say anything."

He reached for her, but she turned away. Instead of letting her go, Cade moved forward, taking her hand with his. "I'm here now, Melanie."

How she wanted to believe that. To think that it could be different—that she could have the marriage she'd dreamed of, and the dreams she'd just achieved. To trust Cade would be there, physically and emotionally, when she needed him.

But if there was one thing Melanie couldn't take, it was more disappointment.

"Cade, it's too late," Melanie said. "We drifted apart. I became your personal assistant, not your wife. And then, when it looked like I might have my chance, you wanted to put me right back into the same box I was trying to climb out of."

"All I wanted was a family," he said. "How can you hate me for that?"

She reached out, touched his hand, but then retreated. Each of them had been hurt that night, but instead of coming together, they'd ended up on opposite sides of a common fence. "I never hated you, Cade. I just wanted to go down a different road."

"You've never told me why, Melanie," Cade said, coming around her, forcing her to face him. "*Why* did you leave me?"

Melanie sighed. Why couldn't he just let their marriage die? "I told you. A hundred times over the past few years, but you never listened."

"I'm listening now. Tell me what it is, so I can fix it."

She threw up her hands. "That right there, *that's* part of the problem. You can't fix everything, Cade."

"I can fix this, Melanie. Give me a chance."

For a second, she wanted to do just that, but then she thought back to the dozens of times they'd had conversations that echoed this one. Things would change for a week, maybe two, and then Cade would go back to being Cade, relying on Melanie to do everything but live for herself. When she'd finally had her chance, all he'd wanted to do was return to the status quo.

She shook her head, then crossed the room, her keys in her hand. She held open the door, waiting for him to exit before shutting and locking it. "No, Cade. You can't fix this."

Then, before she did something really stupid, like revisit that kiss, she turned and went home to her empty apartment, her stomach as disappointed as her heart.

An hour later, Cade walked into the offices of Fitzsimmons, Matthews and Lloyd, although Fitzsimmons had died ten years ago and Lloyd last summer, leaving it technically just Matthews. Even though it was late on Sunday night, he found his father exactly where he'd expected him to be—behind his desk.

The imposing office had been a major part of Jonathon Matthews's life for forty-plus years, and it showed in the dark paneling, the heavy furniture, the deep, plush carpeting. Every inch of the room reflected Jonathon's personality, his high expectations.

When Cade entered the room, his father barely looked up from the brief he was reading. Jonathon had aged well, the only concession to his sixty years a pair of glasses that he wore when no one was looking. His gray hair was cut short, his suit tailor-made. The same attention to detail that marked his office wore well on every inch of the man.

"Cade," his father said, laying the brief aside. "Glad you came in. I wanted to talk to you about the Tewksbury case."

"I'm not here to work, Dad." The look of surprise on his father's face told Cade he'd spent far too many weekends here. "I wanted to talk to you." He slipped into one of the two claw-foot chairs facing his father. "I'm taking next week off."

"Off?" his father echoed, surprise in his tone, his brows arched above the gold frames. "What could possibly be more important than the Tewksbury case?"

"Melanie." Cade swallowed. "I'm going to go work in her coffee shop this week."

The silence in the room was as heavy as a steel beam. "You're *what?*"

"Going to—"

"I heard you the first time." His father scowled. "What the hell are you thinking?"

"I'm trying to save my marriage."

"At the expense of this firm. She's divorcing you, Cade. Let her go, for God's sake."

"She's my wife."

Jonathon waved a hand in dismissal. "You can always get another. A hell of a lot easier than I can find a lead attorney on this Tewksbury mess."

Anger boiled inside of Cade. He knew, since

the day he'd told his father Melanie was pregnant, that the marriage had been a disappointment, a detour from the path Jonathon had planned for the son he saw as the heir to the firm. "Is that how you look at wives? Interchangeable?"

"That's how I look at the ones who walk out on their husbands for no good reason." His father dipped his head, attention on his work again.

But just before he dropped his gaze, Cade saw a flash of vulnerability in his father's eyes. A sheen of hurt, that had lingered despite the perfectionist paint job his father had applied to himself.

"Because Mom did it to you?" Cade said quietly, touching on the one nerve that ran through all three Matthews men.

The sore spot made Jonathon scowl and pick up the brief again. "I have work to do.

And so do you, if that pile on your desk is any indication." But his voice had lost its punch.

"Answer me, Dad." Cade leaned forward. "Is it because she left you with two five-year-old boys and never came back?"

His father shook his head, dismissing the glistening in his eyes. Because it was too painful? Too hard for Jonathon Matthews to admit failure? "All that's ancient history."

Cade wasn't going to let that history die. After all these years, he and his father had never talked about that October day when Elaine Matthews had packed up her station wagon and headed to California. "Your mother is gone," Jonathon had said to his twin boys, before introducing the new nanny in the next breath, as if the whole thing was nothing more than a shift change in the Matthews household.

"After she was gone, you poured yourself

into work, leaving nannies to raise us. Hell, half of them were so bad, we raised ourselves because you weren't there."

"I had to provide for my family."

After marrying and parenting his own child, Cade understood his father better. How would it have been for Cade if he had lost Melanie when Emmie was a little girl? Would he have done the same, retreating into the predictability, the quiet of work?

"Or was it because you had to escape two little boys with a whole lot of questions?" Cade looked at his father and saw himself in twenty years. The thought didn't bring Cade cheer. "And here I followed in your footsteps, right down to the hours at work."

"Law is a consuming business."

"It doesn't have to be. I can have a family and a career."

His father whipped his glasses off and

tossed them to the side. He squeezed at his eyes, erasing the trace of emotion. "What are we living in, fairy tales now? You have a commitment to this firm, to ensuring that our clients are taken care of. If your wife couldn't understand that—"

"She did, Dad. More than any one woman should have had to."

"I didn't make you put those hours in, Cade," Jonathon said. His gaze connected with Cade's. A look of regret flickered in his eyes, then was quickly whisked away. "Before you throw stones at me, you better damned well look at your own garden." His father settled the glasses on his nose again and returned to the brief, to the comfort of work. It had always been Jonathon's escape, and sadly, it was now also his entire life. "Bring me the Tewksbury file, please and we can strategize for court."

Cade bit his tongue before he lashed out. He knew from experience that the only way to deal with his father was calmly and with a good argument. The minute Cade raised his voice, Jonathon would tune him out. "I told you, Dad. I'm working with Melanie this week. Todd can handle my cases."

His father shook his head, negating the idea. "I need *you* here."

"It's only a week, and then I'll be back. Surely the firm can live without me for a few days."

"We probably can," his father conceded. Then he laid his hands flat against the smooth surface of his desk and leveled his steely gaze on his son. "The point is you've been...distracted lately. I put up with it after Melanie left, because every man is entitled to some time to get over a thing like that."

"A thing like that? We were married nineteen years."

"But then," his father went on, ignoring Cade's words, "you didn't snap out of it. You've been about as useful around here as a puppy."

"I've always given you my best, Dad, you know that." The best years of his life, the best weekends, the best nights. Cade had nearly killed himself, putting in long hours, always trying to please his father, to achieve some impossible standard.

And for what? Cade still didn't measure up and never would. Pleasing Jonathon Matthews was like trying to fill an endless, empty well.

"Have you?" his father asked. "Because there have been rumors. That you're talking to Bill Hendrickson about leaving."

Cade blinked in surprise. "Yes, that's true."

"When were you going to tell me?" A flicker of hurt ran through Jonathon's blue eyes, then disappeared. For a moment, Cade wanted to relent. He knew his father had always thought his son would step into the role of heading the firm, but Cade didn't want this life. Didn't want to sit in this office at sixty because his house was emptier than his heart.

"I just wanted to look at my options," Cade said.

"Options other than working for me."

"Yes."

Jonathon Matthews gave one short, brisk nod. "Fine. Then you might as well leave now. Save me from wondering when you're going to drop the ax."

This was what frustrated Cade the most about his father. His inflexibility. Either you measured up or you didn't, and if you didn't, Jonathon was quick to sever the ties. "Dad—"

"You've disappointed me, Cade," Jonathon said, rising and pushing his chair back into perfect alignment with the desk. "I expected much more from my own flesh and blood."

"You've expected *everything* from me!" Cade shot back. "I've given you nineteen years, Dad. Nineteen years in a job I never really loved."

"You could have told me that before I paid for law school. Saved me the money," Jonathon said. "And now you're leaving me, just like she did."

"I'm not her, Dad. And the sooner you stop taking out her sins on me and Carter, the better off we'll all be. Hell, we might even be happy." When his father buried his head in his work again, refusing to open that door of vulnerability again, Cade turned and strode out of the room, unemployed—and wondering if the mess his life had become was beyond salvageable.

CHAPTER EIGHT

ON MONDAY MORNING, Melanie opened the shop a few minutes before the usual 6:00 a.m. start. Emmie, never an early riser, rarely worked the morning shift. Usually Melanie was here alone until about ten. Between the busy bursts, she liked the moments of quiet in the shop, the regulars who stopped in before work.

The bell jingled and Melanie turned, expecting to see Max, the owner of the bakery on Fourth Street. He provided the more complicated baked goods—bagels, doughnuts and cheesecakes—that rounded out her food case.

But it wasn't Max. And it sure as heck wasn't a bagel.

It was Cade, looking too handsome for a man who was at work before the sun finished breaking over the horizon. Today, he wore a light blue golf shirt that set off the color of his eyes and a pair of neatly pressed khakis.

Who had ironed them? Cade? The dry cleaner? Or someone else?

The thought of another woman doing what she had done for more than half her life, for the man she had once loved, slammed into her with a power Melanie hadn't expected.

She'd walked out the door of their house a year ago, intent on starting a life that wasn't defined by being Mrs. Cade Matthews.

She just hadn't thought he'd do the same thing.

Melanie shook off the thought. If Cade dated someone else, or married again, it was none of her business. And it shouldn't bother her one bit.

But it did. Oh boy, did it.

She put on a "I'm not affected by you one bit" smile, but suspected it was as see-through as lace. "What are you doing here?"

"Working," he said, grinning. "Wasn't that the plan?"

"I'd say that plan fell by the wayside yesterday." To be honest, after she'd broken off their kiss and turned down his invitation to dinner, she hadn't expected him to come back.

He put his hands up. "That won't happen again. No more kisses."

"Good." A twinge of disappointment ran through her, but Melanie ignored it. "The morning rush will start pretty soon, so put this on," she tossed an apron to him, the white fabric unfurling as it crossed the distance, "and be ready to latte."

Cade gave her a grin. "Sounds kinda kinky."

She laughed, then sobered when she

realized that once again, she'd be in close quarters with Cade. Considering how well that had gone yesterday, and how much willpower she'd had, she might as well drop her head into a trough of chocolate. The calories from the sweets would be far easier to deal with than what kissing Cade could lead to.

Before she could tell Cade to stay or go—or even more, kiss her again—Max was there with his baked goods, followed by a trio of customers. The morning flood made both of them too busy for the next two hours to think about anything that didn't involve caffeine. Cooter wandered in, got his cup of coffee, then headed for his favorite armchair with his paper and mug.

When the last customer had been served, she turned to Cade. All morning, she'd been aware of him, brushed against him more than once, igniting the same rush of hormones as before. There was no way she could tolerate a week of this.

She shook off the attraction. It was simply that she had been alone for an entire year. The lack of male company made her more vulnerable. It certainly wasn't the way Cade looked, the sound of his laughter as he joked with the customers, or the repartee that had flowed between him and Melanie as easily as milk.

"I know you thought we needed this time together before the reunion," she said, "but really, Cade, I'm sure we can pull off being married for a couple of hours without any additional 'practice.'"

"Oh, yeah?" He quirked a brow at her. "How about we try it for ten minutes?"

"What do you mean?"

He gestured toward the front door of the

shop. "Because Jeanie Jenkins is just getting out of her car and coming into the shop."

"This damned place is busier than a garbage truck full of flies," Cooter muttered, shuffling his paper to the next section.

"Jeannie?" Melanie wheeled around. An older version of the Jeannie that Melanie re-membered was indeed, getting out of an ille-gally parked silver Benz, striding up the walkway and toward the shop. She was as thin as she had been in her cheerleading days, and still sported the same long, curly hair. Even her clothes were more fitting a twenty-year-old than a near forty-year-old. If Melanie hadn't seen her face, she'd have thought Jeannie hadn't aged a minute since high school.

"Melanie!" Jeannie exclaimed, bursting through the door with outstretched arms, as if spying Melanie was like stumbling upon an oasis. She hurried across the shop and grabbed Melanie from across the counter, gathering her into a tight hug.

"Jeannie," Melanie said, pulling back to inhale after that octopus grab. "What are you doing here?"

"Why seeing your little coffee shop, of course! I just couldn't stay away once you told me about it." A gossip finding mission, more than anything else, Melanie suspected. Jeannie toodled a wave Cade's way. He gave her a hello back.

Melanie had thought she'd have a week to prepare for appearing in public with Cade— not to mention a killer dress to boost her confidence. But standing here in jeans, a T-shirt emblazoned with the shop's logo and an apron that had a chocolate syrup stain on the front did little to boost her self-confidence. Or make her feel like half of Westvale High's equivalent of Romeo and Juliet.

Melanie put a smile on her face, then grabbed a mug from the clean ones on the shelf behind her. "Can I get you something?"

"Sure. Something non-fat, decaf and sugar-free." Jeanie waved a hand vaguely. "Whatever you have that does all that and tastes good."

A tall order, but Melanie did her best, combining skim milk, sugar-free caramel and almond syrups with a couple shots of decaf espresso to make a nicely flavored latte. Jeannie dumped in three packets of artificial sweetener, then took a sip. "This is great. Who knew you could do all that with a few beans?"

"Lawford's a couple hours from Westvale. I'm surprised you drove that far for a cup of coffee, Jeannie," Melanie said, doing a little fishing of her own.

"Oh, it wasn't just the coffee. I'm also here for a Stickly." She took another petite sip.

"A what?"

"Stickly table," Jeannie explained. "There's this little antique shop in Mercy, which is, like, really near here. Wait…Mel, don't your grandparents own an antique shop?" Jeannie grinned. "Maybe they'd consider beating the Mercy shop's price."

"They used to own one. Right in this space, actually. But when they passed away, I turned the space into Cuppa Life."

"Oh," Jeannie said, clearly disappointed all she was getting out of the visit was some free coffee. "Too bad. I'm *totally,* like, wild about Stickly. I've been looking for ages for a table to finish off my house and then wham, there was one, in this month's issue of *Antiques.* I was up for a road trip, and then I remembered you had this shop here, and then before I knew it, like, here I was!"

"It was nice of you to stop in," Melanie

said, wondering how long Jeannie planned to stay, because having Cade standing right next to her had Melanie's pulse skittering. If she inhaled, she knew she'd catch the notes of his cologne—a woodsy scent that had played its music in her heart for years. "Quite the surprise."

"I agree." Cade slipped an arm around Melanie's waist, drawing her inches closer. He pressed a kiss to her hair, soft, gentle. The wall around Melanie began to crumble. She found herself leaning into him, wanting more, wanting to believe this was real—

And not an act for Jeannie.

"Aw, you guys are still so sweet." Jeannie sighed. "I swear, all the good guys are taken."

Melanie didn't answer, just smiled back. Cade clutched her tighter, but as the reality of Jeannie's words hit her, she quit believing this was real. This was, after all, their trial run.

In the end, she'd have her building and Cade would have his job in Chicago. A win-win, he'd called it. Even if right now, it felt like one of them was losing.

"That reminds me." Jeannie grinned at them over the rim of her cup. "I didn't just drive out here for a table and a java. I have *another* ulterior motive. I'm killing three pigeons with one, like, tree."

"An ulterior motive?" Melanie echoed.

"Susan and I were talking the other day and we thought how cool it would be to bring back everything we loved about high school. Like, definitely not the teachers or that awful Algebra torture, but the good stuff." Jeannie grinned, then sipped at her coffee before continuing. "Especially prom night. I mean, everyone's going to be in fancy dresses and suits anyway, so we thought we'd recreate that whole, like, prom thing."

Prom night had been the night Melanie had lost her virginity to Cade. The night they'd made love, and in their youthful rashness of forgotten protection, ended up with Emmie. It was the night that had turned the tide of her life, and though she would never want to give back Emmie, she would have loved to change the way that night had turned out.

"I'm not so sure that's a good idea, Jeannie," Melanie said. "Not everyone had a great experience at prom."

"Well, that's where you guys come in." She leaned forward, eyes glittering with excitement. "You're going to be prom king and queen. Get the crowd all revved up for the whole thing."

"Us? But—"

"Oh, but you *have* to," Jeannie said, laying a hand over Melanie's. "You two are the only ones who are still together, at least of the couples who met in high school."

"What about Jerry Mitchell? Wasn't he with Danielle?" Cade asked.

Jeannie waved a hand. "They broke up ages ago. Something about Danielle having a backup plan."

"Most people have backup plans." Cade sent a glance Melanie's way.

"Yeah, but Danielle's backup plan was to wait for a better offer." Jeannie arched a brow. "From a younger man. A waiter at that. I mean, if you're going to toss a husband aside, at least trade *up*."

Melanie shook her head, thinking of the kid who had sat behind her in sophomore English and complained his way through diagramming sentences. "Poor Jerry."

"It's okay. He's been hitched to someone else for, like, two whole years now. Beat my record already." Jeannie took another tiny sip, so small it would take her an hour to finish the coffee. No wonder Jeannie was so thin. She ate more like a bird than a human. "So anyway," Jeannie went on, "we were thinking you and Cade could be the reunion king and queen. Lead us in the first dance, the toast. All that stuff."

Dance with Cade? This was going way beyond a speech. It meant taking their happily married act to a whole other level. Melanie had intended to go in, help Cade with Bill, make the speech, then leave. Not hang around for a reenactment of The Finest Moments of Cade and Melanie. "Jeannie, I don't—"

"We'd be glad to," Cade said, his arm around her waist feeling so familiar, so warm…

And way too easy to fall into.

"We really can't—" Melanie cut in.

"Oh, please," Jeannie said, hands clasped, eyes as wide as a baby beagle's. "You have to do it. Like, everyone is counting on you."

Guilt—the kind that seemed to come attached to every woman's psyche—forced a reluctant agreement past Melanie's lips. "Okay, but—"

"That is so awesome!" Jeannie blasted, her words riding roughshod over Melanie's. "You two will be, like, the whole reunion." She took one last sip, then rose and sent a two-finger wave at Melanie and Cade. "See you all on Friday night. I need to get my Stickly home!"

Then she was gone, hustling out the door as quickly as she'd come in, her nearly full coffee sending up a final curl of steam.

"Well," Cooter said, rising out of the armchair and plopping his hat on his head, "wasn't that a little bit of vinegar in your honey?"

With that, Cooter left the shop—leaving Melanie and Cade alone. Cade's arm still lingered around her waist, as if he'd forgotten he'd put it there—or fallen into old habits. She wheeled around, causing his touch to drop away. "What were you thinking? We can't play the happy couple all night. We were supposed to meet with Bill, make a speech and get out of there."

He scowled. "It's a dance, Melanie, not a lifetime commitment."

"Is it, Cade? Because it sure seems to me that everything you're doing is designed to get us back together." She shook her head, thinking of how many times she'd come close to doing exactly that this week. How easy it would have been to believe that a few days of making lattes together could solve everything. "It's not going to happen."

"And why is that, Melanie? Don't tell me it's because you don't love me anymore." He took a step closer, his hand going to her jaw.

"I don't." But she couldn't meet his gaze.

"So when you kissed me, you didn't feel anything at all?"

She didn't deny or agree. Melanie might be strong enough to stick to her guns on the divorce, but she wasn't strong enough to deny she hadn't felt a thing in that kiss. "You can't build a marriage on a kiss, Cade."

"No, we can't." His jaw hardened, his frustration clear as he released her. "But we can sure as hell try instead of giving up."

"Is that what you think I did? Give up?"

"You walked out, Melanie. I wouldn't say that was fighting for us."

"I fought for us for nineteen years, Cade. And where were you? At work. On a business trip. Anywhere but with me and your family."

"My job—"

She threw up her hands. "It's always been your job. Your career. What you needed. It was never about me. A marriage takes two. It means *both* people have their needs met."

"But isn't this," he said, indicating the

coffee shop, "the need you wanted me to meet? Supporting you in your business?"

"It was part of it, yes."

"And I'm doing that. I'm here, working with you. I'm cosigning on the loan. What more do you want?"

She tore off the apron and tossed it to the side, sliding out from behind the counter. To keep her hands busy, Melanie folded the newspaper Cooter had left behind, fluffed pillows, picked up a couple of stray napkins. "I want a man who knows me. Who knows what I like. What my favorite color is. What I dream of for the future. Who I am, not what he thinks I am."

Cade was there, his hand over hers, stopping her from grabbing a forgotten paper coffee cup, forcing her to face him. "I know all that."

"No, you don't, Cade," she said, yanking away from him. "You stopped paying attention a long time ago. Or you wouldn't have asked what you did that night."

Emmie was striding up the sidewalk and toward the shop. Melanie grabbed her purse and coat, and headed out the door at the same time her daughter headed in. "I'm going to the store to pick up more milk," she said, knowing there were four gallons still in the fridge, but needing to get away from Cade and the conversation more than she needed to replenish her dairy products.

Cade waited a good ten minutes before he started picking Emmie's brain. "Your mom really loves this shop, doesn't she?" he began.

Emmie let out a gust. "Dad, I'm almost twenty years old. If you want to pump me for information, you can get right to the point."

He chuckled. "You've always been too smart for me."

She grinned at him. "No, I just inherited a little of that lawyer gene."

He laughed again, proud as hell of his daughter. She had always been able to hold her own in any argument, often winning over her parents when it came to getting the keys to the car or extending her bedtime. During the teen years, there'd been days when her smarts and argumentative spirit had been a nightmare more than a plus, but that had ended as she aged. "Okay, yes, I wanted to see what you knew about your mom."

Emmie started brewing a fresh pot of decaf. "I don't know why you're asking me. You should be asking Mom."

Cade looked toward the door where Melanie had exited a few minutes before. "I tried that."

"Mom's easy, Dad. Just listen to her."

"I'm trying, Em, but she's not talking."

"Maybe not with words, but she *is* talking."

He poured himself a cup of coffee, then

leaned against the counter and looked at his daughter. "What's that supposed to mean?"

"It means," Emmie said, running a hand through her short, red-tipped hair, "that everything that is important to Mom is in this room."

He looked around the space, feeling as clueless as if he'd stepped into a foreign country where he didn't know the language and didn't have a handy travel guide. Had it gotten that bad, as Melanie had said, that he couldn't discern much about his wife from a room? From her own business?

"Looks like I have some work to do," he said.

"I'll say," Emmie muttered. But in her eyes, he saw the glisten of tears. She gave a one-shoulder shrug, as if she didn't care, but he could tell she did. "I hope you guys work it out, Dad."

"Yeah," Cade said on a sigh. "Me, too."

CHAPTER NINE

THE NEXT FEW DAYS with Cade were business only, which was exactly what Melanie told herself she wanted. Yet even as she watched him move around the shop, interacting with the customers, brewing up their favorite blends, she wanted him. Wondered if their next kiss would be as good as the last one.

When business slowed down on Friday afternoon, she went outside to straighten Cuppa Life's patio furniture. When she was done, Melanie looked at her building for a long minute, then at Ben's shop next door, and its hand-lettered For Sale sign, put up just the other day. As she watched, Ben reached in the window and took the sign down, sending a friendly wave Melanie's way. She'd made her offer yesterday, with tentative bank approval, which Ben had said was good enough for him.

Cade had left to pick up Emmie, whose Toyota was once again putting up a fuss and had broken down two miles from the shop. Once they returned, Melanie and Cade had an appointment with a local bank, to find out if she had received her loan or not.

Given the loan officer's enthusiasm on the phone yesterday, Melanie figured it was probably a done deal—and clearly Ben believed that, too. She'd done it—albeit with Cade's credit score as a boost and their combined savings as well as the house in Indianapolis as collateral—and now she could watch her business become all she'd dreamed. After a year or two, maybe she'd be doing well enough to open a chain of locations. Indiana, Ohio, Pennsylvania—those states were just catching the coffee craze and would make great choices for additional locations.

Melanie had no doubt she could capture a segment of that market, given half a chance. That thought made her excited about the future. She could do this—and do it well. Success with Cuppa Life represented so much to Melanie, and also she knew, to her grandparents, who were undoubtedly watching from above with a smile.

She sighed, missing their calm wisdom, their kind, encouraging words, and most of all, the summers she'd spent here. Not to mention the respite those months gave her from the hectic, messy house in Westvale where she'd spent her childhood. A house where Melanie was often forgotten by her scatterbrained mother and her solitary father.

"We're back," Cade said, striding up the sidewalk with Emmie at his side. Emmie had her book bag over her shoulder, heavy and bulging with homework.

As she watched him stride ahead to hold the door for her and Emmie, Melanie realized how much she'd started looking forward to Cade's arrival. She'd gotten used to him being here, and knew when Monday dawned and he went back to the law firm, there'd be an empty spot in Cuppa Life.

And in her.

"How was school?" Melanie asked as the three of them headed inside, feeling oddly like the family they used to be, or rather could have been, had Cade been home often enough.

Emmie shrugged. "Okay. Though I'd rather watch cockroaches mate than sit through another of Professor Beach's World History lectures."

Cade laughed. "Glad to see our dollars are funding a good education."

"How's Liam?" Melanie asked. Emmie had broken off a year-long relationship at the end of high school and ever since, had been dating casually. It was pretty sad, actually, that her daughter had ten times the dating experience that Melanie had. But she was glad to see it. The last thing Melanie wanted for her daughter was a rush to the altar and a slew of regrets later in life.

"He asked me to go to the movies tomorrow night." Her eyes shone, the excitement clear in her voice, her face.

"He's the one from your Psych class, right?" Cade said.

Emmie nodded, clearly pleased that her father had, indeed, been listening.

Melanie looked from Cade to Emmie, surprised. All the years they'd been married,

Cade had been pretty oblivious to Emmie's day-to-day activities. On any given morning, he couldn't have named her favorite cereal, the boy who'd given her that all-important first kiss, or who was taking her to the prom.

She and Cade had joked about being ships that passed in the night, but after a while, Melanie got tired of being another buoy in Cade's busy life.

"You guys have been talking," Melanie said, as Emmie headed to the rest room.

"It's hard not to when we're working together." He watched his daughter's retreating form and smiled. "She's a great kid, isn't she?"

"Yeah." Melanie grinned. "And it's nice to see her attitude improving this week as well."

"I missed a lot with her," Cade said, then sighed. "I should have been here more. Spent more time with her."

Melanie could have jumped on him then,

pointed out the mistakes, the weekends he'd spent at work instead of at school events, or the business trips he'd taken, leaving Melanie to help Emmie with a science project on tornadoes. But she didn't.

Regret swam in his dark blue eyes, coated every syllable. Instead of recriminating, Melanie stepped forward and laid a hand on Cade's shoulder. "There's plenty of time ahead," she said softly.

He nodded, mute.

"Working here was one of the best things you could have done to get to know Emmie," she went on. "When she was a little girl, we had some of our best mother/daughter conversations in those odd moments. Like riding in the car or folding laundry."

"You and she always had that closeness," Cade said, turning to his wife. "It made me feel like an outsider sometimes."

Melanie blinked in surprise. "It did?"

"When I came home, I always felt as if I'd walked in after the punch line of the joke," he said, his gaze on some distant point in the past. "You and Emmie are like two peas in a pod."

"She was an only child, Cade. That meant all she had was me." Melanie realized what she'd just said and hurried to make it up. "I meant, you weren't home that much and—"

"I know what you mean." His attention swiveled back toward her, and in that second, a memory slipped between them, written in that unspoken mental language of longtime spouses. "It almost wasn't that way, though, was it?"

"Cade—"

"Are we ever going to talk about it, Melanie? Or just pretend that it never happened?"

She waved toward the back of the shop. "Emmie will be out any second now."

"Fine," Cade said. "But we have to talk about it sometime."

"Sure," Melanie said, intending no such thing. That day had been painful enough. Cade's absence, her guilt. There was enough fodder there for a soap opera.

"Mel, didn't you want the baby, too?" Cade asked, his voice just above a whisper.

She turned away, straightening mugs, aligning the handles until they were like little circular soldiers marching along the shelf. "I can't talk about this."

"Can't or won't? It takes two to kill a marriage, you know. And two to bring it back to life."

"I don't want to bring it back to life," Melanie said, wheeling around. "I don't want to go back to being Suzy Homemaker."

"When did I ever say you had to do that?"

"Last year," Melanie said, "standing in this

very space. I said I wanted to run my own shop and you asked me how I could possibly do that if I had another baby. You just assumed I wanted to try again. Assumed I wanted to go back to being a housewife and a mom. Assumed I wanted to put my dreams on hold one more time."

The rest room door squeaked as Emmie opened it and both Cade and Melanie let the subject drop. A couple of students wandered in, followed by two men in suits who took a corner table and flipped out their laptops.

Cooter ambled in next. He tipped his cap Melanie's way and ordered his usual. His light blue gaze flicked between Cade and Melanie. "That old dog, he's still whining from what I can hear," Cooter said, taking his mug. "And there ain't nobody happy when the dog's not happy."

Cade gestured toward Cooter as the old man headed to the back of the shop. "What'd he mean by that?"

"He told me a story about some dog that got sick eating mulch or something." She shrugged. "I don't know, it's supposed to have meaning for my life."

"Mulch? And a dog?" Cade chuckled. "Jeez, if I'd known the secret to life was that easy, I'd have brought home a golden retriever and landscaped the front beds."

Melanie laughed, glad for the break from the tension of their earlier conversation. Emmie joined them, looking from one parent to the other. She smiled. "Good to see you guys getting along so well."

"Oh, we're just—"

"Sharing a joke," Cade intercepted. "Nothing more."

"Uh-huh," Emmie said, clearly not believing them. "Either way, you two better get out of here. Don't you have a meeting?"

"I almost forgot!" Melanie slipped off her apron, grabbed her coat and purse off the hook inside the kitchen. "I'll see you tomorrow, Em."

Emmie smiled, her gaze again split between Melanie and Cade. "Have a good time tonight."

Hidden meaning—work those marital problems out on the dance floor.

"Thanks for taking my shift, honey," Melanie said, ignoring the hint to get back together with Cade and instead laying a quick kiss on her daughter's forehead. Emmie gave her mother another eye-roll, but didn't move away. Despite her being well past the age when kisses were dispensed with the abandon of confetti throwers, Melanie was convinced Emmie still secretly liked the occasional tender touch. Even if it was from her mother.

The shop door jingled and Liam entered, his

attention more on Emmie than Cuppa Life's offerings. "Hi, Liam," Emmie said, a soft, private smile curving across her face.

"Hi, Em." He slipped onto a stool and returned her smile.

"I think that's our cue to go," Cade whispered in Melanie's ear.

A thrill charged through her at the feel of his warm breath along her neck. She closed her eyes for a half a second, giving up to that feeling, before dismissing it. The bank loan, the reunion, it was all part of a business deal. Not a date. There wasn't going to be some miraculous happily ever after created while the band played "Always and Forever."

Even if a tiny part of her was starting to hope otherwise.

Cade stood in his kitchen, wrestling with the black bowtie that went with his tux.

Carter leaned against the wall, watching his twin with clear amusement. "Need some help?" he asked.

"No. I can get it."

Carter arched a brow, then glanced around the messy kitchen. "This place is really starting to scream bachelor. You gotta do something."

Why was everyone telling him that? He *was* doing something—it just wasn't working. He'd thought, after the meeting with the bank this afternoon, that things might change. That the minute the loan officer said, "Congratulations," Melanie would have turned to him, and called this whole divorce thing off. But she hadn't. Instead she'd thanked him as politely as she had the bank manager, then told him she'd see him tonight.

It couldn't have been more businesslike if they'd been standing in a boardroom.

"Did you come over just to complain about my decor?" Cade said to his twin.

"Nah. I was hungry, too. You have anything to eat around here?" Carter opened a cabinet, rifled through it for a second, then turned back to his brother. "Are you sure you don't want some help with that tie? It's a mess."

Cade threw his brother a glare.

Carter just laughed. "All right, but don't blame me if you end up looking like a guy who wrapped his own Christmas present." He moved some cans of green beans, found nothing behind them, then shut the cabinet door. "This is sad. Old Mother Hubbard had more than you do, Cade."

Cade hadn't eaten at home in so long, he couldn't remember what he had on hand—if anything. "Check the fridge. There might be some leftover Thai food."

Carter rose, opened the Whirlpool and

withdrew one of the paper takeout boxes. He took one whiff, then shoved it back inside the refrigerator and slammed the door. "You need to fix things with Melanie, man, before you die of e-Coli or typhoid or something."

"My vaccinations are up-to-date," Cade said with a grin. "And I'm making progress with Mel."

"How so?"

"I worked with her at the coffee shop all week."

"Five days serving up lattes? Should have been enough time to solve your problems, the world's problems *and* have some time leftover." Carter grinned.

"You don't know my wife."

"Neither, apparently, do you, if you couldn't get her to talk." Carter opened the freezer, but found only several inches of frost and one pizza box that had started to curl at the corners.

He shut the door again, fast. "Did you ever try to figure out why she won't talk to you?"

"Because Melanie is more stubborn than a herd of donkeys."

"Or maybe because she *is* talking and you aren't listening."

Cade started in on the tie again. That was the same thing Emmie had said. "What is that supposed to mean?"

"All along, you've been saying it's her that won't talk. Saying she's the one who walked out on the marriage. Did you ever think that it might have been you?"

"That's insane. I've always been there." The final bow tightened against his neck and he turned around. "Well, except when I was at work."

"And how great of a husband do you think Dad would have been if he'd married again?"

"Dad would have been horrible. Heck, he

wasn't even good at the father thing. Never home, always talking about the office, leaving us to do our own thing."

"Uh-huh. Do you recognize anyone in that picture?"

Cade shook his head. "I'm not like Dad."

"You are, too. You're just not as crabby as he is." Carter grinned. "And you don't share his opinion that I'm an idiot."

"He just wants you to make something of yourself." Cade had served as the go-between for the two for years, but he might as well have been a brick wall, given how little Carter and their father communicated. Cade wondered sometimes if his Type-A, workaholic father envied Carter's footloose approach to life.

"I did make something of myself," Carter said. "What I made wasn't good enough. He wanted me to be a lawyer. I'd sooner commit hari-kari than spend all day locked up with legal briefs." Carter snorted at the very idea. "Do you even *like* being a lawyer?"

Cade sighed and dropped into one of the kitchen chairs. "No, I don't."

"Then why the hell are you doing it?"

"Because Dad paid for me to go to college. Gave me a job when Melanie and I had nothing. No money, no apartment, nothing but a baby on the way."

"And he's made you pay him back ten times over," Carter said, sliding into the opposite seat. "If you hate your job, quit."

"I don't have a backup plan, Carter. It's not like I can take my law degree and be a really good bartender."

"You took your law degree and made really good coffee. Mixing a margarita on some beach in Jamaica should be a piece of cake after that."

Cade laughed, then returned to reality. To a

mortgage, college tuition and a retirement to fund. "I'm not going to throw away a twenty-year career to serve women in bikinis."

"You have got issues, my brother." Carter chuckled. "I'd do just about anything to serve women in bikinis."

"That's why you're the bachelor and I'm the—" Cade cut himself off. He wasn't the married one, not really. "Okay, bad point. Still, I'm not applying for any jobs in Jamaica."

"There may be an opening as a toy company CEO soon if I keep helping this business run into the ground," Carter said, then glanced at his watch. "Anyway, I have to go. I have a date." He rose. "I may be a bachelor, and a disappointment to my father and a guy whose still trying to figure out who he is, but at least I'm honest about it. One piece of advice. The sooner you get honest with yourself, the sooner you can get honest with Melanie, too."

Then Carter left, leaving Cade with a mental mirror finally large enough for him to see the reflection of himself. He got out a piece of paper and began to write.

CHAPTER TEN

"Last time I saw you in one of those, it was light blue," Melanie said. "You looked like the Easter Bunny."

Cade chuckled. "If you prefer the blue…"

"Oh, no. the black is nice." Maybe too nice because she had to remember to breathe. She noticed everything about him, especially the way the tux framed the muscles and planes of Cade's body. Every hormone in her body itched to undo the tie, then start on the tiny black buttons, unfastening one after the other until she got him down to his boxers—

And nothing else.

It was a major change from the business casual he'd worn to the bank earlier. True to his word, Cade had stayed quiet throughout the loan process, letting Melanie run the show—and collect the check at the end. Cuppa Life was going to finally fulfill what Melanie had envisioned, which made her excited about the days to come.

But right now, the only thing increasing her pulse was Cade and the sexy cut of the fancy black suit.

"You look amazing." The compliment shone in his eyes as much as it did in his tone. Cade took a step forward, then reached out and ran a finger along the thin strap of her dress. "Absolutely incredible."

Her breath caught in her throat, her gut twisted with a want that had never seemed this strong, this overpowering. Before she could think about what she was doing,

Melanie closed the gap between them, lifted her chin and pressed her lips to his.

He groaned, then his arms stole around her waist. He pulled her to him, hard and fast, nearly catching her breath in her throat. She knew all it would take would be one word—no, one glance—and she and Cade could be in her bedroom, undoing all they had so carefully done to get ready for tonight.

"Oh, Melanie," he said against her mouth, his voice heavy with want, need—the same river rushing through her veins, begging for release.

"We should…go," she breathed in the space between their lips, not wanting to go at all, not wanting to do anything but keep on kissing him.

"Yeah."

But neither of them moved.

"I want you," he whispered. "I've always wanted you. From the first time I saw you, there's never been anyone but you, Mellie."

"Cade—"

He put a finger to her lips, shushing her protest. "I've never wanted another woman and I never will."

"We should go," she repeated, but everything within her rebelled against the thought. Of leaving what was happening right now unfinished. "We should go…" and then, the need for him conquered her doubts, and she took his hand. "To my bedroom," she whispered, ignoring the warning bells rung by common sense, heeding only the need that tightened and curled inside her gut, a call that knew exactly how Cade would answer.

"Oh God, Melanie," he said, his voice nearly cracking. He scooped her up, cradling her to his chest, his lips drifting across hers in a soft, sweet caress. Melanie wrapped her arms around his neck, craving more of this, craving him, needing him to fill that empty space inside her.

"I want you, too, Cade," she said.

He pulled back to look at her, his eyes filled with the gentle kindness that was quintessential Cade. "Are you sure?"

She nodded. "First door on the right," she whispered as he headed down the hall, her hands going to his bow tie. She tugged it loose, then worked her way down the tiny black buttons of his shirt, anxious to feel his skin beneath her palms, the sure strength of Cade against her body.

He deposited her gently on the bed, then kicked off his shoes. They landed with a clunk, matched by the twin sound of her heels following. Electricity filled the air, charging the space between them. His mouth on hers was hungry yet still tender, his hands warm and tight on her hips. He lowered himself beside her, their bodies carving together as easily as two puzzle pieces.

She worked his shirt out of his waistband, flicking the last two buttons out of their fasteners, then tugging it down and off his arms. She paused a moment, allowing herself the agonizing pleasure of running her hands along his chest, feeling the planes and muscles she had memorized over the years. He was familiar, and yet new, after all this time apart, and she marveled at the warm hardness beneath her palm.

Their mouths met, a ravenous kiss that tasted lips, tongue, every inch of each other. Cade tugged her dress up and over her body, then paused, his gaze softening as it swept over her body. "I've had this dream many times over the last year."

"Oh, yeah?" She grinned, teasing him. "And how did it end?"

He leaned down, trailing kisses along her neck, between her breasts, skirting the lacy edge of her bra. "Let me show you," he said, his voice nearly a growl.

An instant later, Cade was fulfilling her with the knowledge of a man who had had twenty years of learning his wife's body. He touched all the right places, stroked at just the right pace and sent every one of her nerve endings into another stratosphere.

She ran her hands down his bare back, urging him to quench a thirst that had suddenly become unbearable. He kissed her neck, her breasts, everything he could reach, while her palms explored his firm, amazing body.

It was familiar, yet as new as the first time. Their crescendo built quickly, fueled by the year apart, and before she knew it, she was crying out Cade's name in concert with him. When the sensations finally ebbed, Cade rolled to the side and pulled Melanie into his arms. She couldn't remember feeling warmer, or more secure.

"I love you," he whispered.

Those same three words lingered on the tip of her tongue, but as she came back to reality, Melanie held them inside and pretended she hadn't heard Cade. She couldn't say them back. Because in the morning, all of this would go back to what it had been. Once before, Melanie had lain in Cade's arms, sure that everything would change, then been shattered when it didn't. She couldn't bear to go through that again.

Instead she raised herself onto one arm and glanced at her bedside clock. "We're going to be late."

The magical spell between them dissipated.

"You're right." Cade released his hold on her and rolled away, clearly hurt.

And broke the spell.

He slipped on his clothes while she did the same, neither of them speaking. When she was done, Melanie fixed her hair in her dresser mirror. In the reflection, she saw Cade wrestling with his bow tie, cursing under his breath. "Let me do that," she said, crossing to him.

His dark gaze riveted on hers, making her fingers jumble her first attempt at the tiny silk neckpiece. She dipped her gaze and concentrated on the tie, finally getting it back into proper order. "You're all set."

"Thanks." Cade reached up and brushed a tendril of hair away from her face, weaving that magic around them once again. For a long moment, neither of them said anything.

Melanie tore her gaze away from his. "We have to go."

Cade nodded, disappointment clear in his features. Together, they headed out of the room, the bed linens as tangled as her emotions.

Melanie grabbed her clutch purse from the bench by the door, then walked with Cade out to his car. He opened the passenger's side door—something he had never failed to do in nineteen years of marriage—then waited until she was seated before shutting it and coming around the other side.

"I've missed that," she said when he got in the car.

"What?"

"Someone opening the door for me."

Cade only murmured an agreement before he started his Volvo.

Melanie slid a glance his way. The second the statement left her, she'd expected that he would say something about how she could have him opening her door every day, if only she'd take him back. But he hadn't.

Had that moment in her bedroom been a final fling between them? His "I love you" more of a goodbye than a return to the old days? And if it was, why did that thought send a little shiver of disappointment through her?

During the two-hour ride to the hotel hosting the Westvale High reunion, Cade kept the conversation impersonal, sticking mainly to the subject of buying Ben's building and her plans for the expansion.

He'd clearly been paying attention—to her thoughts, her business ideas. "Thank you," Melanie said.

Cade flicked a glance her way before returning his attention to the road. "For what?"

"For listening."

"I'm making up for lost ground," Cade said. "With Emmie, and with you. And while we're on the topic, I've been meaning to thank you. For letting me work at the shop this week. I really enjoyed it."

She chuckled. "I'm sure those cappuccino

skills will come in handy when you go back to Fitzsimmons, Matthews and Lloyd."

"Yeah, I'll have to get a machine for the break room." He cast his gaze toward the road before them for a moment, then back at her. "I needed that opportunity to do something else. I've worked for my father for nearly twenty years and never had as much fun there as I did in your coffee shop." He reached for her hand, gave it a short, tight squeeze. "You've accomplished so much with your coffee shop. I'm really proud of you, Mellie."

Something softened inside her, giving room for hope to expand its reach. "I appreciate that," she said softly. "I enjoyed having you there, too, this week. Except for Ben, I haven't really had anyone to talk to about the business."

He glanced at her again. "You miss your grandparents, don't you?"

Tears sprung to her eyes, and she nodded, surprised that he had read that in her.

"They'd be proud. Really proud, honey."

Melanie whisked away the tears that dropped from her lashes. "You're going to make me ruin my makeup."

"You'll still be beautiful," Cade said, his words seeming a hundred times more intimate in the darkness. "You do a great job with that shop, Mel. You have just the right mix of location and atmosphere to make it work."

She sat back against her seat and studied him. "I never expected you to say that."

"The truth isn't so hard to say." He grinned.

As Melanie watched the world pass by in a muddled blur of inky night and spots of light, she had to wonder whether that was so.

When they walked into the gaily decorated ballroom at the hotel that was hosting

Westvale High's reunion, several people hurried over to Melanie and Cade, calling their names. Even after so many years apart, Cade recognized several of the faces, but was still damned glad the reunion committee had stuck name tags on everyone's chests.

"Paul Klein!" Melanie exclaimed, striding forward, Dave at her side to greet their old friend. At six foot six, he still towered over Melanie, even if his long curly hair had become a buzz-cut. "How have you been?"

"Great, great," he said, giving Melanie a warm hug, before turning to shake Cade's hand. "It's been a long time since those double dates in Cade's Mustang, huh?"

"You guys are *finally* here!" Jeannie enveloped them in a double hug, then pulled back to indicate a trio of class officers behind her. There was a flurry of introductions, of catching up. Somehow, Cade lost track of Melanie, separated by the flood of people.

Then, he caught sight of her, standing to the side, chatting with a brunette whose face rang a familiar bell; Cade didn't remember her name. He wasn't aware of anything really, except for Melanie. In that deep crimson dress, with her hair loose around her shoulders, Melanie managed to pull off both sexy and elegant, the fabric skimming down her curves, making him wish it was his hands running along those feminine lines again.

Their lovemaking had been as intense as it had been in those early days when passion overrode every thought, and yet this time, it had the added depth of years of connection. Cade had thought—hell, prayed—that in the afterglow, Melanie might have been tempted to try again. But her silence when he'd said he loved her spoke more than anything else she'd said in these last few days.

Melanie was right. One kiss, or even a hundred kisses, wasn't enough to rescue their marriage. Making love to his wife had only been a temporary mask for their problems.

On the way over here, he'd intended to play by her rules. To keep it cool and impersonal, but the longer she stayed in his sight, the more impossible it became, especially as his mind replayed the moments in her bedroom, the sweet ecstasy of having his wife in his arms again.

Still, if he rushed her, or he pushed too hard, he knew he could end up driving her away. His fists clenched at his sides, keeping him from reaching for her, drawing her back into his arms. Then she smiled at him, and something within Cade tightened.

Maybe it was the starry lights strung

overhead, the way the disco ball above had been adapted to sweep a sparkling of light across the floor. The soft music, the band crooning a ballad from the eighties…

It was as if they had stepped back in time. Cade slipped through the crowd, weaving in and out among the people until he reached his wife. He slipped his hand into hers. Comfort infused him.

"Cade," she said, her voice a warning.

"For just one night," he whispered, not wanting to let go of the veil of intimacy temporarily surrounding them, "let's pretend nothing has gone wrong. Let's just be Cade and Melanie."

She cocked her head. "Wasn't that the plan, so that no one knows what's going on?"

"I don't care what other people think. I want us to forget those papers on my desk, to forget it all, and go back to the beginning."

"But…" Her voice trailed off, as if she were about to reject the idea as easily as she had his whispered confession of love earlier.

"In the morning, we go back to business as usual," Cade said, wishing that wouldn't happen, praying that tonight had turned the tide between him and Melanie. "For tonight, Mellie, just tonight, be my wife. One more time."

She hesitated, then her green gaze met his, and she nodded, her gaze dropping to the ring on her finger. "One night. Like Cinderella."

The band segued from a fast-paced song to a slow and easy ballad. Cade may be surrounded by people whose names he'd long forgotten, but he recognized the familiar notes. The Whitney Houston hit whispered its magical melody, flashing his mind back to late nights in his Mustang, parked wherever they could grab a little privacy, the windows fogged from the steam of young love, while the radio played those same melodic strains. "They're playing our song."

"You remembered," she said, clearly surprised and touched that he recognized it.

He nodded, his gaze locked with hers, searching, still searching, for those lost threads of his marriage. "Dance with me, Mel."

"But I see Bill Hendrickson over there." Melanie pointed to where the punch bowl and appetizers had been laid out. Bill stood beside the cheese platter, chatting with two other men. He sent a wave Cade's way. "Didn't you want to talk to him?"

"Later. Right now, all I want is to dance with you." Cade reached out, waiting until she'd put her other hand in his, then, together, they made their way to the dance floor. As it had in the days before work and nighttime feedings and dirty dishes had taken over their days, the music made the world around them drop away. He swept her against his body, one arm around her waist. Their pulses merged, heartbeats synchronizing with their every step.

She tipped her head up, her eyes dark and unreadable, her lips inches from his. Want brewed inside him, a different and deeper want than what he'd felt earlier tonight. It was as if, at this moment, with Melanie in his arms and the music of their past playing in the background, his life had finally come full circle.

And everything within him was rebelling at the thought of giving that up.

"Kiss me," she whispered. "Kiss me, Cade."

A smile curved across Cade's face, then he dipped his head, and brought his mouth to hers. She tasted of berries, a sweet dessert. She slipped her arms around his neck, bringing them closer, closing in their world even tighter.

"That's *exactly* why you guys are king and queen!" Jeannie exclaimed. "Because you are, like, the ultimate couple."

CHAPTER ELEVEN

JEANNIE'S LAUGHING VOICE brought the real world crashing back. Melanie stepped back from Cade. "Hi, Jeannie."

Cade didn't offer a greeting. Instead he mentally cursed the former cheerleader's timing.

Jeannie sighed. "You two are *so* Adam and Eve. I wish I had a man like Cade. I mean, not the real Cade," she laughed, "because he's, like, taken, but one who looks at me like that. It'd also help if he had a really high credit limit. Oh, and definitely a Porsche." She grinned, then took both their hands, pulling them from the dance floor. "Anyway, I'm really sorry to interrupt a little marital fun, but it's time to give your speech."

Cade had practiced his speech all afternoon in his head, mentally weighing the combination of a typical welcome with something a little more personal—and that might get Melanie's attention.

Jeannie led Melanie and Cade up to the stage, leaving them in the shadows of the side curtains while she charged over to the microphone, as hyper as a two-year-old. "We're all, like, so excited to see so many Westvale High people! It's totally a rush to see us all together again! But let's get right to it and bring out the couple you've all been wanting to see, our reunion King and Queen, Cade and Melanie Matthews!" Jeannie started clapping, her face bright and eager. She waved at them, gesturing the two forward.

"Are you ready?" Cade asked Melanie.

"As ready as I'll ever be." But her voice shook on the last syllable.

"You'll do fine," he said, then took her hand and strode onto the stage. As soon as they reached the microphone, Jeannie hurried to a nearby stool, grabbed two silver plastic crowns and plopped them on Cade and Melanie's heads. Cade smirked at Melanie, who gave him one of Emmie's eye-rolls back.

"Thank you all for coming," he said into the microphone, withdrawing a sheaf of papers from his inside pocket and smoothing them onto the podium. "On behalf of the class officers, I'd like to welcome you to our twentieth reunion. Jeannie asked Melanie and me to talk about the passage of time—and about how some of us have stayed the same while others have changed, like by putting on a few pounds." At that he patted his stomach, which elicited a burst of laughter. "Don't worry,

Dwight," Cade said to the former football captain standing in the front row, "I won't be tackling you tonight. I can't afford the hospital bill."

Another round of laughter.

"But one thing I can tell you that has stayed the same in all those years—" at this he turned briefly to Melanie "—is how we feel about each other, how we feel about those people who were—and still are—closest to us. The years may have aged us, but they have also aged the friendships, the connections, we built up over the years. Those have only grown in depth, even if we now live miles apart."

Melanie felt the words, heard them in her heart. She knew her husband wasn't talking about Bill, Paul or Dwight or any of his high school friends, but of her.

Had those years really intensified their feelings for each other or driven them further apart? She looked at the crowd below them, seeing pairs of best friends who had been separated for years and then picked up as if they'd never been apart. Tonight, she and Cade had done the same in her bedroom—only with a lot more va-va-voom.

Was it possible that the foundation she and Cade had built all those years ago was still there, waiting for them? Or was she imagining it, still caught up in the afterglow of their lovemaking?

"Our job," Cade continued, "tonight and into the future, is to maintain those connections. To not let the busyness of our lives or the focus of making it through today distance us from those we love and who love us."

Someone in the audience hooted agreement.

"And with that, I'll introduce my lovely wife," Cade said.

The word startled Melanie. How long had

it been since she'd heard Cade call her that? Tears threatened at her eyes, as she realized that once the paperwork was filed, she'd never hear those words again.

Cade turned away from the podium, and as he did, the papers in his hand slipped from his grasp, fluttering to the stage floor.

Melanie bent to pick them up. A smaller piece, different in color and shape from the typewritten pages, slid out of the pile.

A list. In Cade's handwriting. With her name at the top, as if she were a task he had to complete. She saw the words "shop, bank loan, baby," before Jeannie scooted in, gathered up all the papers and shoved them at Cade.

"Hey, we got, like, big-time dead air," she hissed at Melanie. "You have to do something. Say your speech."

Before Melanie could react to what she'd just seen, she found herself at the microphone, unfolding the handwritten pages holding her speech.

The spotlights above her gave the ballroom a sense of being an enormous black hole, an endless sea filled with people expecting a few words of wisdom from the reunion Queen.

Even if she didn't feel like she had any to give.

"I look at the passage of time a little differently from Cade," she said. In her mind, the words on the list flashed in front of her, a trio of warning signals. How could she have been so foolish? To think that things could actually change? "But then again, I'm a woman, which means I rarely agree with him. And of course, when it comes to arguments, I'm always right."

Laughter erupted from the crowd.

"Maybe it's because I'm a mom. When you have a baby, it seems as if the days—and most of the nights—are endless." She paused for another ripple of laughter. Melanie was grateful to have a written speech in hand, which allowed her to keep her mind on speaking, instead of what she'd just seen on that scrap of notebook paper. "But then, you look back and one day realize the years have passed in a blur, and everything around you has changed. I see the years in our wrinkles, our thighs—" at that, she patted her own "—and in our conversations. Where we once talked about who Adam Garvey liked—" she indicated the former hottest guy at Westvale, who'd become a balding veterinarian "—we now talk about our children and how it terrifies us that they're dating. We used to focus on taking tests, now we chat about keeping our jobs. And yet, one thing is still a common topic. The future.

"We look ahead, as we did twenty years

ago, and hope that we have made the right decisions. That we will take the paths that lead toward our goals and our dreams. Sometimes, those paths take us in different directions. But in the end, I'm confident that we can all sit around a table, put on the coffee, and in that, find common ground again with those we love." She thanked the crowd and took a step back from the podium.

The crowd erupted in applause. Cade tossed her a grin as easily as a Frisbee. Melanie turned away, unable to look at him without seeing that list.

"That was just totally awesome," Jeannie said, taking over the mike again. "And now, for the couple of the night—and the most happily married people I've ever seen—we have a special prize." She pulled an envelope out from behind her back, then handed it to Melanie, at the same time tugging Cade closer. "A totally romantic weekend away in windy Chicago, provided by Hartstone Travel." Jeannie leaned forward, increasing her vocal volume. "Hartstone, making travel fun for all ages. And a special thank you to Jim Hartstone—" at that, a chubby guy in a suit took a bow, while Jeannie led a round of applause "—for this great gift."

"Uh, Jeannie," Melanie said, trying to interrupt Jeannie's continued effusive thanks for Jim. The envelope in Melanie's hands weighed heavy with the knowledge that it would never be used, at least not by the Mr. and Mrs. Matthews scrawled across the front.

No matter how romantic it might have been to tango with Cade in bed, to waltz under a faux starry sky, to twirl around the dance floor in his arms, she was fooling herself if she thought Cade would ever change. He'd made that clear tonight, when she'd found that list.

"*Jeannie,*" Melanie said again, louder.

But Jeannie kept on, touting Jim's company as the next best thing to owning your own cruise line, while the band played a soft melody beneath her voice. "I wonder if Cade and Mel are still limber enough to use the champagne glass hot tub. Not that you two need the extra spark," Jeannie said with a grin that seemed tinted a little green with envy. "Everything about you two is just perfect, isn't it?"

"Ye—" Melanie cut off the yes before it could come out. She was done agreeing to keep the peace, to make someone happy, to preserve the status quo. Done with pretending to be something she wasn't. She placed the envelope on the podium. "No, Jeannie, it isn't. And we can't take this gift. I'm sorry."

"What?" Jeannie cupped her hand over the mike. Behind them, the band screeched to a stop. "What did you just say?"

"Mel, it's okay," Cade cut in. "We'll settle this later."

"When, Cade?" She wheeled around. "When are we going to get to the point and quit fooling ourselves that one night in bed, once dance or even a weekend in Chicago—"

"With a destination package valued at six hundred dollars," Jeannie cut in with a hopeful, work-with-me smile.

"—will bring back what we used to have. It's not going to happen, Cade, because we are getting *divorced.*"

A hush rippled through the crowd. Cade's face paled, as if finally speaking the words in public made them irrefutable. Jeannie gripped the mike stand, her face about three shades below death, and swayed a little. *"Divorced?"* she squeaked.

Silence descended its heavy blanket, muting the merry atmosphere of the reunion. The word seemed to echo, carrying through the room, drumming home the reality.

Melanie and Cade—divorced.

And then, it hit her, too. Hard and deep, like a punch to the gut that she'd forgotten to steel herself for. She'd moved out, filed the papers, started over in Lawford, but throughout it all, the actual thought of divorce hadn't seemed as real as it did right this moment.

She and Cade were finished. She would never again feel his hand in hers, his lips against her mouth, hear his voice warm against her ear.

Melanie was giving up her husband. And in doing so, Melanie wondered who the real loser was.

"Got a lawyer yet, Mel? I'm a real shark in the courtroom." She glanced out at the crowd, searching for the voice, but could see only the flash of a white business card against the dark backdrop.

"I'm sorry," Melanie said, then she ripped the crown off her head and escaped the stage.

"Melanie, wait!" Cade called after her, his long legs closing the distance between them quickly and reaching her just as she exited the hotel. "Why are you leaving?"

She spun around. "I don't want what you want, Cade. We're only hurting each other if we keep trying to make this charade work."

"What do you mean? We made love tonight, Melanie. After that, I thought things were going to be different, that maybe a door was opening between us."

"So did I, but I was wrong." She looked away, her gaze going to the wide, white moon, hanging low in the ebony sky. "And I'm sorry about what happened back there. I probably ruined it for you with Bill Hendrickson."

He waved a hand in dismissal. "It doesn't matter. I already turned down the job."

"You did? Why?"

"Because I can't leave you." He grinned, that same familiar smile that held a special place in so many of Melanie's memories. "I can't go to Chicago and walk away from us. You go ahead and file that divorce, Melanie, if you really want to, but I'm not letting go that easily."

She shook her head. "Cade, I didn't want to bring in lawyers—"

"I didn't mean I would fight you in court. I meant I'd fight you here." He reached forward and pressed a palm to where her heart beat.

She thought of the list. Of the third item Cade had on it. How tempting it would be to give in to the emotions stirred up by those moments beneath the sheets and on the dance floor.

She shoved the feelings aside. It was crystal

clear, especially after she'd seen the words in Cade's own handwriting, that his goals were miles apart from hers. "Don't, Cade. We want different things. Just let it go."

"I can't." His gaze locked on hers. "I love you, Melanie. I always have."

"Oh, Cade, please don't make this difficult." Tears burned behind her eyes. She loved this man—she was fooling herself if she ever thought she could stop loving him—but Cade deserved a woman who would give him what he wanted.

And that woman wasn't Melanie, not anymore.

"I'm not making anything difficult," he said, moving closer, taking her hand. "Unless you count kissing as more difficult." He leaned forward, his mouth a whisper from hers.

How easy it would be. But tomorrow,

Melanie knew, she'd be back to where she was before and breaking it off a second time would be ten times more painful.

She jerked back. "Don't."

Surprise filled his blue eyes, tinted with hurt at her rejection. "You can't tell me you stopped loving me, Melanie. I saw it in your eyes tonight, felt it when you kissed me. We're meant for each other and whatever problems we have, we can work them out."

The thought tempted her. How easy it would be to believe they could go back to being the Cade and Melanie they had been twenty years ago.

"Tell me you love me, Melanie," he said, "and we'll start all over again, right here."

If she said those words, her life could go back to what it had been before. The problem was, Melanie no longer wanted that life.

"I don't love you anymore, Cade." A single

tear fell from her lashes, but she held her gaze steady on his. "I'm sorry."

Cade stood in the hotel parking lot while cars came and went and the world moved on, Melanie's words slamming against his heart like a wrecking ball. He'd hoped, no, prayed, that it wasn't too late. He'd always believed, beneath it all, Melanie still loved him.

He would have given anything to hear her repeat what he'd said. To have her, one more time in his arms, her lips meeting his with desire, her body curved into that same familiar place, against his heart.

He could have fought her, argued back, lashed out and released all the hurt wrapped around his chest like chains. But he couldn't do that to her.

He swallowed hard. He had to let her go, even as every ounce of his soul protested. "Then I guess that's it." He inhaled, then let the breath out again with two words. "Goodbye, Melanie."

Cade turned on his heel, and left behind the only woman he had ever loved.

CHAPTER TWELVE

MELANIE WATCHED CADE WALK away, her heart shattering. She'd just told the biggest lie of her life.

She sunk against one of the columns supporting the entryway to the hotel, burying her face in her hands. When she did, the memories washed over her, unstoppable. The two of them, welcoming Emmie into the world. Singing lullabies late at night. Cuddling on the sofa. Eating popcorn while a rented movie played on the television and she and Cade got reacquainted after another business trip.

When had she quit believing in that love? In them?

"Mel, you okay?" Jeannie exited the hotel, the hem of her floor-length dress gathered in her hand as she navigated the stone entrance in high heels.

"Yes," Melanie said, then drew in a breath. "No."

Jeannie laid a hand on Melanie's arm. "Do you need a ride home?"

"Are you sure you don't mind?"

"Not at all." Jeannie dug in her jeweled purse for a set of keys, then dangled them in front of the valet, who hurried off to retrieve her car. "If there's one thing I'm good at when it comes to relationships with men, it's making an escape."

Melanie asked Jeannie to drop her off at Cuppa Life. The whole ride back to Lawford was filled with Jeannie's endless chatter about the people at the reunion, a full-out gossip fest that any tabloid columnist would have relished. This time, instead of being annoying, Melanie enjoyed the endless one-sided conversational stream, if only for the distraction.

"Thanks, Jeannie," Melanie said when the car stopped in front of the shop. She paused to look at the woman she'd hardly known in high school but now, ironically, counted among her friends. "You're a great friend and I'm glad you talked me into going to the reunion."

"It was nothing," Jeannie said, then swiped at her eyes. "This whole reunion has me, like, all emotional. It's either that or I'm PMSing."

Melanie laughed, then exited the car, promising Jeannie a free nonfat, noncaf coffee any time she wanted it. As Jeannie drove away, Melanie dug in her clutch purse for the keys to the shop. The entire downtown strip was silent, all the businesses locked up for the night, including Cuppa Life. Melanie let herself in, then turned on one light in the back of the shop. She made some decaf, poured a cup, then sank into Cooter's favorite armchair, kicking her high heels to the side.

The bell over the door jingled and Melanie leaped to her feet, half expecting Cade. Cooter stuck his familiar head inside the door. "You serving coffee?"

She chuckled. "Only decaf. Technically I'm closed. But I'd be glad to get you a cup."

"I could use it. A man my age has trouble sleeping. I decided to take a walk, see if some fresh air might bring on Mr. Sandman but I think he left for the Bahamas." Cooter slipped onto one of the bar stools, thanking Melanie for the mug she slid his way. "You take care of that dog yet?"

It took her a second to figure out what he meant. "Sort of."

"Is it still hurtin'?" He watched her over the rim of the mug.

Did it still hurt?

Absolutely. Ten times more than the day she'd walked out on Cade. Now, the end of their relationship was truly final. She almost wished they hadn't had this week together because it had made that last goodbye nearly unbearable. "Yeah," she said. "It hurts."

"Then why the hell are you still eatin' the mulch?" He took another gulp of coffee, then tipped his hat her way as he stood. "You have a good night now, Mrs. Matthews."

When Cooter was gone, Melanie lingered at the counter for a long time, thinking about what he'd said. She busied herself with straightening the shop, wiping tables that didn't need to be wiped. Going home to her empty apartment was too depressing of a thought.

The bell jingled again. Melanie, in the middle of drying Cooter's mug, called out. "We're closed."

"Did you mean what you said back there?"

Melanie wheeled around, nearly dropping the wet, slippery mug. "Cade."

"Did you mean what you said on the stage?" he persisted. His bow tie was undone, along with the top button of his shirt, his jacket probably back in the car. He looked tired and yet, at the same time, determined. And yet, as always, he stopped her heart.

"About what?"

"About us finding a common place, even if our paths have diverged?"

Melanie looked at the man she had loved more than half her life. She wanted to say yes, but couldn't. If there'd been common ground for her and Cade, she had missed it.

"You know speeches," she said, a burning behind her eyes so fierce, she had to blink it away, "you make up stuff that sounds good on paper."

He crossed to the counter, then slipped behind it, once again seeming to consume the space between them. "I don't believe you."

She stepped back, surprised by the strength in his words. "Cade, I told you it was over."

"I heard you. And I'm not giving up that easily. I let you walk out a year ago and I didn't put up a fight. I kept thinking you'd be back. You needed a little time and then you'd change your mind. But you didn't come back. If anything, you got further away from me— from us. And if I let you walk away again, I'd be a fool."

She put the mug on the counter, then wrapped her arms around her waist to keep from wrapping them around him. "I saw the list, Cade. I saw what you expect out of me."

"The list?" It took a moment before the light dawned in his eyes. "That wasn't what you thought. It was—"

"No, Cade." She put up a hand to stop him. "I know you. You talked a good game to me this week about *my* goals and *my* dreams, even complimented me on the shop, but all you really want is for me to go back home and play housewife while you go out and conquer the world."

"You don't really think that, Mel. I don't want to lock you in the house with an apron."

She tossed down the dish towel. "How the hell do you know what I think? You barely know me, Cade."

He scowled. "That's not true. I know you better than you know yourself."

"Then you should have known the last thing I wanted was to have more children." She exited the kitchen, around the counter and out into the coffee shop, grabbing her shoes and slipping them back onto her feet.

Cade followed, grabbing her arm to make her stop and face him. "That's not what the list was about, Melanie. It wasn't a list of what I wanted for the future, it was a list of things we needed to talk about. And while we're on the subject, what would be so bad about having another child? We always wanted more than one."

"No, Cade. *You* wanted more than one. I wanted a life after I was done raising Emmie. I had her so young, I never got to do anything." Melanie shoved her feet into her shoes, ignoring the pinch at her toes. "I was in that damned apartment all day long, changing diapers, heating bottles and watching my life pass by in a blur of play dates and dirty laundry. And what about you?" She flung out her hand, indicating an imaginary globe, a world that had spun past her, while Cade circled it day after day for his clients. "You were off, traveling the country, enjoying fancy lunch meetings, interacting with *grown-ups,* while the little wife was at home singing along with Big Bird." She drew in a breath, calming the flare of anger in her chest. "I love Emmie, don't get me wrong, and I wouldn't have undone those years with her for a million dollars. But I also—"

She broke off the words and turned away, the tears no longer hiding behind her eyes, but streaming forward, down her cheeks, a burst watershed.

"Also what?" he asked, his voice gentle, concerned.

She shook her head, mute.

"What, Mel?" Cade asked again, tipping her chin up until her gaze met his. "Tell me. *Please.*"

"I resented her," she said finally, the words cracking as the truth exploded from her, coated with guilt that any mother could ever feel that way. "And I resented you. I was *eighteen,* Cade, and my whole life was over. That wasn't the way it was supposed to be."

"You don't think I thought the same thing, honey?" His voice was as ragged as hers, the hurt, the blown chances, all shattering in his words. "I went to work for my father, and stayed there, because a man provides for his family. He doesn't run off on some silly notion that he could be an artist or a musician. He *provides,* Mel. Whether he likes it or not." He drew in a breath, his eyes closing for a second. "I resented the way our lives turned out, too, but I was afraid to say anything."

"Because a man doesn't show weakness, either," Melanie finished, adding another of the lessons Jonathon Matthews had drilled into his sons' heads. No wonder Cade had always been Can-Do, and especially Can-Do Alone. He'd been brought up to shoulder all the weight and never, ever admit a weakness.

"Do you know why I picked apart your coffee shop idea that day?"

She shook her head.

"Because I stood here, in this very space, hearing you talk about your idea for a coffee shop, and all I could think of was how jealous I was of you."

A plane flew overhead, the muted sound of the engine cutting between them for a moment. "Jealous? You? Of what?"

"You knew what you wanted, Melanie, and exactly how you were going to get it. All of a sudden, you had freedom. Choice. I realized I had spent twenty years at my father's law firm and never *ever* felt what I saw in your face that day." He gripped her hands, his touch warm and secure. "After I worked with you this past week, I realized I couldn't go back to law again. So…I quit my job."

The words hit her with surprise. "You quit

working for your father? You mean so you can go work for another firm, right?"

"No, I quit law altogether."

If there'd been a game show with the question "what would Cade be most likely to do?" Melanie would have never guessed that. Cade had been more driven and committed to his career than anyone she'd ever known. "But you love what you do."

Cade's gaze met hers, seeing in her green eyes the distance that still existed between them and the price he had paid—they all had paid—for a career he'd never truly enjoyed. "No, I don't. Corporate law was my father's dream. Not mine."

Melanie shook her head, confused. "But you never said anything. You put in all those hours and spent all those weekends at work. Why would you do that if you didn't even like law?"

Cade sank into one of the armchairs, then

waited as Melanie took the one opposite. "In my family, you don't complain. You do your job, you do it well and then you come back for more the next day. One day turns into another, and before you know it, years have gone by." He paused and let out a heavy sigh. Finally admitting he was done with practicing law had released a twenty-year-old weight from his chest. For the first time ever, he wondered what was around the corner of his future. "I wish I could have a do-over for those years. I never meant to let the job take over our lives. I never meant to become my father. I looked at him the other day and saw what that life has cost him. He's given up everything, probably because he was afraid of being hurt again, because my mother leaving really did a number on him." Cade shook his head, knowing it might be too late for his father to realize there was a life waiting for him, but it wasn't too late for Cade. For Cade and Melanie. "I won't use work as a wall anymore. And I won't let that become me."

For nineteen years, they had argued about his hours, about her frustration that he'd never been there for the important moments. That his father had gotten more of Cade than Melanie and Emmie ever did.

But now, Melanie understood her husband in ways she hadn't before. She looked around the room and realized she and her husband had more in common than she'd thought. "I get it now, Cade. After a year of running my own business, I've seen how easily work can consume a person. In my case, it's because I'm pretty much everything from bookkeeper to bottle washer. I haven't had time to get a manicure, much less have a relationship. You become so immersed in the job, you forget to live, too."

He nodded, and that thread of understanding between them twisted and thickened into a rope. "And here I went into law because I thought it would *build* the relationship I'd never had with my father. Somehow please the unpleasable Jonathon Matthews. I thought he'd look at me someday and tell me I'd done the right thing. But mostly, I did it because I hoped working in his firm would give us time together. Something we never had when I was a kid."

"And it didn't," Melanie said, already knowing how much Jonathon and Cade had worked, their endless schedules leaving no room for recreation or building a bridge between father and son. She reached out, laid a hand on Cade's arm, knowing from her own childhood how much a person could still crave that parental relationship even when they were long past the age of wanting cookies and conversation after school. "I'm sorry, Cade."

He shrugged. "I guess I pictured us going on these father-son fishing trips or some such idiotic fantasy. But we never did. Dad worked as much as he always had, if not more. And I—" he let out a breath "—I fell into the same trap. What's worse, I *became* the very person I didn't want to be. I worked too much, I saw you and Emmie too little, and in the end, it cost me everything that really mattered." He reached for her hand and squeezed it. "I'm sorry, Melanie."

But the apology wasn't necessary, not anymore. She held onto that rope of understanding, wondering if maybe it was enough to hold them together. "Cade, that's how you are. You're a Type-A. Success at all costs. I can't blame you for that. Besides, part of it was my fault, too."

He blinked. "Your fault? You didn't make me go to work."

"No, but I didn't speak up, either," she said, finally being honest with herself and with him. It had been far too easy all these months—heck, all these years—to just blame Cade, instead of face her own shortcomings. "I realized that tonight, on the stage, when I almost agreed with Jeannie's plan, even when it wasn't what I wanted to do. I'm a yes-man, or woman." She let out a bitter chuckle. "And I was in our marriage, too. I argued about the missed soccer games and the dinners that got cold, but I never told you how much it hurt me that you were gone. I just went with it all, yes-ing it to death."

"Until last year."

She looked away, her gaze filling with tears. "Yeah, until then."

But he moved closer, undaunted, invading her space, forcing her to look at him. "Why can't we fix that, Melanie? If I'm not working myself to death, and you're not saying it's all okay when it's not, then why can't we fix it?"

"Because it wasn't just about the hours, Cade. There was more than that."

He threw up his hands in frustration. "What more? All I want is for you and I to love each other. For you to be there when I wake up in the morning. I'll do whatever it takes, Melanie, to make this marriage work."

"I *can't* go back to that," she said, rising, her voice choked with tears. The idea of being with Cade again was far too enticing, too easy to fall back into. But if she did, if she returned to his bed, his arms, she knew she'd be unhappy. Maybe not tomorrow or next week, but someday, she'd end up in the same place as before. As much as she had dreamed of returning to what they'd had, she realized now the problem was partly that—what they'd had, even in those early years, hadn't been working. "I lost myself in our marriage. When I slipped that ring on my finger, I expected you to complete me, or something like that. And I thought I would do the same for you. Like some big happy Hollywood ending."

His gaze searched hers, regret shining in those familiar blue depths. "But we didn't find that happy ending, did we?"

"No." She smoothed a hand down her dress. "For twenty years, I invested all my energies into making sure you and Emmie were happy, and in the process, I forgot who I was. I lost the things that mattered to me."

"I never wanted that, Melanie. All I wanted was for you to be happy." His shoulders dropped. "I thought you were."

"I know," she said, softer now. "I don't know if it was because we married too young or if I just let myself get swept up in some fairy tale that wasn't real. It was like our marriage was this delicate crystal ball and I was afraid to tip it or add anything to it, in case it broke." She paused, drawing in a breath, feeling her stomach expand against her palms, knowing she had to hit on that nerve someday or it would keep hurting. "Then, we lost the baby—" The word tore out of her throat, raw and painful over a year later.

Tears shimmered in his eyes, and Melanie reached for him, sharing that loss in a connected touch. Clearly their loss was still an unhealed wound on both sides. Cooter's words of wisdom came back to her.

Get smart enough and you'll stop doing stupid things that hurt you.

Like never talking about the night that had formed the final fracture in their marriage. Like never realize her husband had been as stricken by that loss as she had. She saw it in his eyes, in the hunch of his shoulders, the lines in his face. "Cade, I'm sorry," she said, her voice cracking, "so sorry we lost the baby. And I'm sorry we drifted apart after that, when we should have come closer together."

His eyes met hers, clouded by unshed tears. "All I did was work even more than before. I kept thinking that it would help me get over losing the baby, but it didn't. And…"

"What?" Melanie said, soft, easy.

He let out a sigh. "I thought if I avoided you, we wouldn't have to talk about it."

"I did the same thing." She shook her head at the irony of their common thinking, which had done nothing to build commonality. "Avoiding the problem only made it worse."

He took her hands in his, thumbs tracing the lines of her fingers. "And when you started talking about opening your own business, all I saw was that I was losing you, too."

"We should have talked," she said, wondering

how it might have been different and whether they could have headed off the twists and turns that had followed. They probably should have talked from day one, about the important things, but they'd been young and their marriage hadn't come with a manual. "I guess I thought we'd been together so long, we should have been able to read each other's minds."

"I can't even remember other people's names," Cade said, that familiar grin on his face. "And you thought I could read your mind?"

She chuckled, glad for the moment of levity. "True."

Then he sobered, his gaze going to their connected hands for a moment before meeting hers. "Do you still think it's too late?"

She turned away, swiping at the tears that began to run down her face as her mind flashed the past year in front of her. "I don't know."

"What happened to you that night,

Melanie?" Cade's voice was as gentle as his touch, his eyes dark with empathy and regrets. "We tried for so long to have another child, and then after the miscarriage, you wouldn't even talk about the subject again. You changed."

"No, I realized who I really was." She didn't bother to stem the flow of tears anymore, nor the guilt that had racked her soul for months. "It wasn't just me. Where were you, Cade? Because you weren't there for me. I needed you, but you were gone."

"San Francisco." Cade closed his eyes. "I was in San Francisco."

She leaned against the cushions, her mind rocketing back. Cade, out of town—again—and her hurrying to make it to the dry cleaners before they closed so that she'd have his shirts ready for him when he came home. Emmie in the car, arguing with her mother about something that was unimportant five seconds later. Just enough distraction for Melanie to look left when she should have looked right—to see the SUV running a red light.

She'd woken up in a hospital, the doctor shaking his head, Emmie crying in the chair beside the bed and Cade, unreachable because he'd turned off his cell phone during a meeting with a client.

"I'm sorry, Melanie." Cade drew his wife into his arms, repeating the words over and over, until his voice grew hoarse and the apology finally sank in, a salve for the wounds of the last months. "I'm sorry I wasn't there. I'm sorry I couldn't stop it from happening."

"And then—" She went on, her breath hitching in her throat. She couldn't stop to absorb his touch, his soothing voice. She had to say it and say it now or she never would. "—when the doctor said the accident had done too much damage to my body, you said we could adopt. We'd find a way." She shook her head, thinking of how she had failed, how she couldn't set herself up for that ever again. "I couldn't do that, Cade. I had just inherited this place." She indicated the coffee shop, then faced her husband and the ugly thoughts that had run through her head that night. "And all I could think in that hospital room was how *relieved* I was. That I wasn't going to be tied down. I was free to do what I wanted." Her voice cracked and shattered, and the tears streamed down her cheeks, coupled with a clenching guilt that made her want to run from the room, to hide this other, awful Melanie from him. "What kind of wife feels that way? What kind of mother does that make me?"

"Oh, Melanie, you're entitled to want something for yourself." Cade captured her jaw with his hand.

"Even at the cost of my marriage? No, Cade, I don't agree." She met his gaze, and knew that a lot of things may have changed in the past year—except for one. "I love you, Cade," she said finally, admitting the truth to herself as much as to him, "I always have. But you deserve a woman who wants the same things as you do." She rose, pulling away from him, even as her heart broke with the distance. "Please, just let me go."

"Why? Because you don't want to have more kids? That's not a crime, Mel. And besides—" at that, he grinned "—I'm getting a little old to be chasing after a toddler. I'd much rather chase after you."

The words took a moment to sink in. "You don't want more children?"

"I want *my wife*. My marriage," Cade said. "I meant what I said before. All I've ever wanted is you and Emmie."

"But—"

"Another child would have been a blessing, don't get me wrong. But what would my life be like if I lost you in the process?" His gaze sought hers, holding her there as surely as he'd held her in his arms earlier that night.

"You aren't mad? Disappointed?"

"No, not at all," he said, getting to his feet and pulling her to his chest. She leaned into his touch, feeling as if she'd stepped back in time, to the days when all she'd had to do was love Cade and the rest worked itself out. "I love Emmie and I love you, and if that's all we ever have, that's okay with me."

"But I thought…" Her voice trailed off as this new information filtered in and changed her image of her marriage. Her husband. Suddenly she didn't want to go back to the way it used to be.

She wanted to see what tomorrow would

hold. What this new, and older, Cade and Melanie would be like.

"We both thought we knew what the other wanted. Maybe it's because we met when we were so young. Or maybe because everyone called us the perfect couple. Even perfect people screw up, Mel," Cade said. "And neither of us realized what we were missing until what we wanted most was gone."

"Or when it came back," she said, a smile turning her mouth up, filling the empty spaces in her heart. She ran her hands down his back, feeling the strength in his muscles, the solidity of this man. The only man she'd ever loved. "And insisted on manning the cappuccino machine."

He chuckled. "I haven't been all that good about being there for you before, but I'd like to try, if you'll give me the chance."

She considered his words, meeting the same

familiar blue eyes she'd known since kinder-
garten, loved since high school. "That depends."

"On what?"

Her smile widened. "On whether you know
how to latte."

"Sounds kinda kinky," he said, grinning.

"Oh, it is, Cade, it is." Then she kissed him,
and realized everything she needed for the
perfect brew was already in her arms.

EPILOGUE

CADE AND MELANIE STOOD at the makeshift altar, hands clasped, waiting while the preacher finished his sentence. "I now pronounce you husband and wife. Again." Reverend Martin grinned, then gestured between them. "You may kiss your bride."

"And you may kiss your husband," Cade murmured to Melanie, just before he took her in his arms and revisited another memory.

Behind them, the room erupted in applause and a couple of catcalls. Melanie turned, her face aflame, and laughed. It seemed half the city of Lawford had shown up—and maybe it had, at least the western side. Several of the university students, and even Cooter, stood inside Cuppa Life Deux, the second location in the beginning of what Cade and Melanie hoped would become a franchise. Instead of a ribbon cutting, Cade had suggested a very different ceremony to christen the new location.

"Are you ready, Mrs. Matthews?" he whispered in her ear.

"Ready for what?" Every day with Cade had been an adventure, and she had learned to adapt with this newer, funner man who now shared her business and her life. He'd quit the law firm, opting to spend his days beside Melanie instead. They worked well together, which had given Emmie not only the satisfaction of being right, but enough extra time off to pursue what had become a very intense romance with Liam.

"For a new future."

She nodded, taking her bouquet from her beaming daughter, then strode down the narrow, short aisle, peppered with coffee filters cut out in the shape of flowers.

As they reached the end, Ben gave her a congratulatory hug, his eyes misty. "I'm glad things are going well for you," he said.

"And for you," Melanie replied, smiling at his wife, standing beside him.

"Glad to see you put that dog out of his misery," Cooter said, ambling up to the group.

Cade and Melanie smiled at him, knowing his wisdom—albeit offbeat and often hidden in weird metaphors—had been part of what brought them back together. Cade drew his wife to his side, unable to stop from kissing her again. All this renewal of vows had him feeling as in love as the day he'd first said, "I do."

"If you're done doing what you're doing," Cooter said, indicating the preacher and the altar, "I'd like to try one of those fancy lattes you two keep talking about."

Cade and Melanie exchanged a glance that erupted into laughter. They'd learned how to latte all right, and had plans to keep on doing it.

"Jeez Louise," Cooter muttered as the couple kissed again. "What's a man gotta do to get a cup of coffee around here?"

"Marry the owner," Cade murmured in his wife's ear. "But be sure you win over her heart *and* her espresso machine."

Melanie laughed. The perfect ingredients for her life, her happiness, were all right here. Emmie, the shop, and most of all, Cade.

MILLS & BOON PUBLISH EIGHT LARGE PRINT TITLES A MONTH. THESE ARE THE EIGHT TITLES FOR SEPTEMBER 2007.

❧

THE BILLIONAIRE'S SCANDALOUS MARRIAGE
Emma Darcy

THE DESERT KING'S VIRGIN BRIDE
Sharon Kendrick

ARISTIDES' CONVENIENT WIFE
Jacqueline Baird

THE PREGNANCY AFFAIR
Anne Mather

THE SHERIFF'S PREGNANT WIFE
Patricia Thayer

THE PRINCE'S OUTBACK BRIDE
Marion Lennox

THE SECRET LIFE OF LADY GABRIELLA
Liz Fielding

BACK TO MR & MRS
Shirley Jump

MILLS & BOON®
Pure reading pleasure

0807 Ron

MILLS & BOON PUBLISH EIGHT LARGE PRINT TITLES A MONTH. THESE ARE THE EIGHT TITLES FOR OCTOBER 2007.

THE RUTHLESS MARRIAGE PROPOSAL
Miranda Lee

BOUGHT FOR THE GREEK'S BED
Julia James

THE GREEK TYCOON'S VIRGIN MISTRESS
Chantelle Shaw

THE SICILIAN'S RED-HOT REVENGE
Kate Walker

A MOTHER FOR THE TYCOON'S CHILD
Patricia Thayer

THE BOSS AND HIS SECRETARY
Jessica Steele

BILLIONAIRE ON HER DOORSTEP
Ally Blake

MARRIED BY MORNING
Shirley Jump

MILLS & BOON
Pure reading pleasure

0907 Rom LP

NEATH PORT TALBOT LIBRARY
AND INFORMATION SERVICES

1		25		49		73	
2		26		50		74	
3		27		51		75	
4		28		52		76	
5		29		53		77	
6		30		54		78	
7	10/18	31		55		79	3/16
8		32		56		80	
9		33	7/16	57		81	
10		34		58		82	
11		35		59		83	
12		36		60		84	
13		37	11/16	61		85	
14		38		62		86	
15		39		63		87	
16		40		64		88	
17		41		65		89	
18		42		66		90	
19		43		67		91	
20		44		68		92	
21		45		69		COMMUNITY SERVICES	
22		46	10/17	70			
23		47		71		NPT/111	
24		48		72			